Her Dragon's Heart, Dragon Guard Series #8 by Julia Mills

Her Dragon's Heart

Dragon Guard Series #8

By

Julia Mills

There Are No Coincidences.

The Universe Does Not Make Mistakes.

Fate Will Not Be Denied.

Her Dragon's Heart, Dragon Guard Series #8 by Julia Mills

Edited by Lisa Miller, Angel Editing Services
Proofread by Alicia Carmical with AVC Proofreading
Cover Designed by Linda Boulanger with Tell Tale Book Covers

Her Dragon's Heart, Dragon Guard Series #8 by Julia Mills

DEDICATION

Dare to Dream! Find the Strength to Act! Never Look Back!

Thank you, God.

To my girls, Liz and Em, I Love You. Every day, every way, always.

Her Dragon's Heart, Dragon Guard Series #8 by Julia Mills

HER DRAGON'S HEART
Index of the Words from the Original Language of the Dragon Kin

Teaghlaigh	Family
Draoi	Wizard
Fuil mo chuid fola	Blood of my Blood
Mo dhaoine	My People
A'r ndaoine	Our People
An Dara	Second in Command
Ghealach Dearg	Red Moon
Tost	Silence
Bhaint agus a chur ar ais	Remove and Restore
Mo chroi'	My Heart
Mo ghra'	My Love
M'fhíorghrá	My True Love
Tá tú mo ghrá eternal	You Have My Eternal Love
Ta' mo chroi istigh ionat	My Heart is Within You
Demon ar ríchathaoir	Demon on the Throne

Her Dragon's Heart, Dragon Guard Series #8 by Julia Mills

CHAPTER ONE

"I'm sure you've got a damn good reason for dragging me halfway around the world and then marching me through a swamp in the pouring rain…"

Liam paused and Jace braced for what was to come. He knew there was no way his best friend was done with his verbal ass-kicking. Liam was the Grande Poobah of bitching. He hadn't even reached the path to the pinnacle of his capabilities yet.

"So out with it, asshole, before I call my dragon and head back home."

Jace sighed a heavy sigh. He knew Liam was right. Almost forty-eight hours ago he'd awoken the other Guardsman from a sound sleep, thrown a packed duffle at his chest, and told him to 'dragon up'. True to form, Liam had done so without question, a testament to the strength of their friendship. A bond Jace could tell was wearing terribly thin. The problem was he had no idea how to explain why they were doing what they were doing without giving away his secret…something he'd been hiding since his first trip to the hospital almost four months ago.

One look into her haunting hazel eyes. A mere whiff of the spicy scent of flowering dianthus. Just one moment in her presence and he'd *known*. Could feel it with every fiber of his being. Had confirmation from the beast within… Melanie Whelan was *his*. The one woman in all the world created to complete him and his dragon in every way. Jace had found his mate.

He'd spent the rest of the day in a fog. Not sure what to do or say. His beast had begged for him to throw the beautiful nurse over his shoulder, carry her far from civilization and make her theirs forever. More than a few minutes were spent in debate with his dragon and in all honesty…the big guy had almost won. After a long walk around the hospital grounds, Jace returned to his post and spent the next few hours mooning over his newfound treasure like a schoolboy with a crush.

After a few sleepless nights, Jace had contemplated talking to Royce, the oldest Guardsman of their Force *and* his mentor, but as Fate would have it, things had gotten complicated. They had gotten a lead on the traitor, blown up a mansion, then lost the traitor. They also had a mating ceremony and welcomed the first female dragon in hundreds of years into the clan…pretty much same shit different day for his people. At least nothing was ever boring. It had, however, kept him from doing little more than smiling at his beautiful mate.

Rayne, the Commander of their Force, had tried to remove him from the detail responsible for watching Lance's mate, Dr. Sam Malone, and Jace had come close to losing his cool. His guard detail was the only time he was sure to see Melanie. There was no way he was giving it up without a fight. It took some fancy finagling, but he'd been able to stay on the team *and* see his mate almost every day.

It had taken almost a week, but Jace finally worked up the nerve to have more than a three word exchange with Melanie. The more they talked, the more he realized how perfect she was. Her quick wit and wicked sense of humor were just a few of the things he would never get tired of. He'd always been told the Universe did *not* make mistakes, but it was still the most amazing thing he'd experienced in all his fifty-four years.

The cute way her nose wrinkled when she giggled with the children on the Pediatrics floor or the way her eyes shone when she helped her geriatric patients filled his heart with tenderness. Keeping himself from kissing her silly every time they were together had become a constant battle. Thoughts of claiming her as his own had become an obsession.

The more time he spent with her, the stronger their bond became. He had begun to feel her emotions, even caught glimpses of her thoughts. The intimacy of sharing her feelings was miraculous, something he looked forward to as much as his next breath. So when those feelings just stopped, like someone flipped a switch, Jace MacQuaid *flipped his lid*.

In an instant, he was out of bed, dressed, and flying down the road on his Harley, constantly reaching through their mating link, praying to the Heavens he could catch even the slightest sense that Melanie was okay. The longer her 'radio silence continued, the more his panic grew. It was a new experience for the young Guardsman and one he hoped never to repeat.

Trying to calm both himself and his dragon, he thought back to the last time he'd seen her. She'd been quiet, distracted…almost pensive. Her emotions had become erratic after Kyra announced she had a lead on Calysta involving some whacked out coven of black witches/wizards known as the *Dorcha*, descendants of the Firbolgs – the dark aborigines from the 13th century.

Anxiety flooded their mating bond. Jace probed, looking for the cause of her fear, but Melanie's thoughts were locked up tighter than Fort Knox. Her features so well-schooled that only someone who'd studied her as much as Jace would notice the rigid set of her shoulders and the way she continually glanced to the side.

He'd asked what was wrong and she'd made an excuse about being tired then walked away without looking up. Never one to relent, Jace followed, hoping for answers. Instead, Melanie ducked out of the room, returning several minutes later with her backpack and coat. She made an excuse about an early shift, which didn't fit her schedule and raised more red flags, but the kicker was when she left without letting him walk her out.

Jace paced Royce's front porch until he'd worn a path, then made three laps around the yard before calming enough to go back inside, cursing himself for not making her tell him what was wrong. The notion of *making* Melanie Whelan do *anything* was laughable and made him smile.

I should've told her she was my mate. That we're meant to be together forever. That I'll be there for her no matter what.

Over the next few days there had been countless times he'd on his way to see her, only to have her look up, fake a smile, then head the opposite direction. He knew she was avoiding him but had no idea why. Using every one of his enhanced abilities, he watched from the shadows, undetected but still close enough to protect her.

On the evening of the second night, he'd had enough. He *knew* their attraction was mutual. He'd scented her arousal when they touched, seen her pupils dilate, felt her breath quicken, and felt their connection the few times he'd lowered his lips to hers. Melanie Whelan was his, *dammit,* and he would protect her to his dying breath, whether she liked it or not.

Waiting in the hospital parking lot, determined to get some answers, Jace propped himself against his motorcycle and waited. Her scent filled the air seconds before she exited the large sliding glass doors. He made a beeline to intercept his stubborn mate, reminding both himself and his dragon they were there to get answers, not to be distracted by her sparkling eyes and kissable lips.

Unfortunately, two strides into his trek, the cellphone in the pocket of her scrubs rang. Her steps slowed as she pulled it from her pocket, then stopped completely as she scowled at the display. Biting her bottom lip and staring at the phone like it might bite her, Melanie finally answered with a growled, "I told you *never* to contact me."

The hair on the back of his neck stood up. His dragon snarled. Jace used his enhanced hearing to listen as the raspy voice of a much older man responded. "But Meli Rose, we are family. I just…"

"You just want to screw up my life…*again.* Well, not this time *seanathair.*" The venom of her tone had Jace and his beast preparing for battle. The use of the old dragon language and a blasphemous term like *seanathair* had him scratching his head. Only those well versed in dragon dialect would know what an insult the use of 'old father' would be to their grandfather. He made a note to find out how in the *hell* she was so well-versed in their language.

The sing-song tone laced with malevolent force that replied to her made him want to punch something. "Now,

Meli, you know you belong with your *teaghlaigh*. We know what is best for you."

Melanie transformed before his eyes. Her back went ramrod straight, her shoulders pulled back, and her feet spread to shoulder width apart. A warrior was born and she was preparing for battle. The tension in her jaw worried Jace that she might break a tooth. She growled her response.

"You know what is best for *me*? You? You, *Grand Draoi*, presume to know what is best for *me*?" She paused, her hate and anger a living being.

Although Melanie was truly pissed, Jace *felt* what it cost her to stand her ground. The internal battle to fight for what was right against a blood relative was one that never came easily for anyone. He fought the urge to go to her. His hands flexed with the need to grab the phone from her hands and verbally assault the man that dared to upset his mate. More than anything, he wanted to spare her the obvious torture the mere sound of the man's voice caused.

His beast within wholeheartedly agreed, chuffing and growling until the young Guardsman had a hard time maintaining his focus. Of their own volition, his feet moved forward. Jace ground the heels of his boots into the asphalt, willing himself to stay put. He knew Melanie would *not* welcome his intrusion, no matter how good his intentions. There was history to her torment, something he could tell she'd spent years learning to keep hidden. One of the many things he admired about his mate was her strength and knew from their many conversations that she valued her independence. Watching her, he could see how hard she'd fought to attain that independence and would do whatever he could to help her maintain it. He took several deep breaths, assuring both himself and his dragon he was doing the right thing.

Seconds ticked by as he waited. Melanie stood as still as a statue, her ragged breathing the only signs she was alive. Just when Jace was sure she would hang up without another word, she spoke. The sound so low and ominous, he'd have never believed it was her had he not seen it with his own eyes. His blood ran cold at her words. "Let me guess, *fuil mo chuid fola*. I'm to follow in my mother's footsteps? To carry on the family tradition and die at the end of your sword. Chained to a stone altar, pleading for you to spare my life, only to have you smile and tell me it is for the good of *mo dhaoine*."

"We all do what we must for *ár ndaoine*."

"At least you have the balls to be honest."

"I have never lied to you, Meli."

Her brittle, humorless laughter sent chills down Jace's spine. So different from the beautiful sound of bells he'd come to associate with his mate's laughter that he actually did a double take. "No, you're right, you've never outright lied. Just twisted, omitted, and misdirected until your words bore absolutely no resemblance to the truth."

"Melanie Rose," the old man snarled, his eloquently constructed veneer beginning to crack. "You will listen to me."

The words felt heavy on Jace's ear and were quickly followed by a flair of magic. Melanie's words confirmed its origin.

"Stop with the parlor tricks, *Draoi*. We both know the only reason you're even bothering with me after all these years is that your magic is waning. You need a sacrifice to replenish your power, and not just any sacrifice… but one of your own blood. I'm guessing none of the others have come into their powers yet. Am I right?"

Time stood still. All his focus on Melanie. Worry bounced between him and his beast. They feared she'd miscalculated her grandfather's power. What little Jace knew of magic that wasn't dragon magic was limited, but he knew it took serious mojo to give the kind of mystical push he'd felt a minute ago *through a damned cellphone*. If the old man made a move to hurt Melanie, Jace was ready and more than willing to kill him…wherever the hell the old man was.

"Having a hard time answering a direct question, *seanathair*?" She paused, turning in a complete circle as if looking for someone she knew wasn't there.

Jace had been closely monitoring their surroundings, shocked at how quiet the employee parking lot was for a Thursday night. He knew the closest person was on the other side of the hospital, enjoying a latte on the patio outside the cafeteria, but nonetheless he looked right along with her. When Melanie returned to her original position she inhaled deeply, held her breath to the count of ten, then slowly exhaled. It was obvious she was trying to relieve some tension, and even more apparent, she had failed.

From his vantage point, Jace watched as a sardonic smile lifted the corners of her mouth. Her tone dripped with sarcasm. "No, that's not it at all, is it? You can't find them. Your *teaghlaigh* has abandoned you. They left you with no one but the weakest of the coven and made sure you shared blood with none of them. You're just about tapped out. Karma really is a bitch, isn't She, *Draoi*? That little show of power was meant to scare me? You were hoping I would tuck tail and beg for forgiveness? But the truth is, if you still had power, you would still have your faithful guard, and they would be here to grab me while you provided the distraction. "

She stopped and gave an evil chuckle, which Jace could only imagine infuriated the old wizard. "Well, rot in hell, *seanathair*. I hope…"

Whatever she was about to say was extinguished by the boom of thunder and a bolt of lightning that not only lit the sky but landed inches from Melanie's feet. As the asphalt before her smoldered, Melanie screamed, "You will not win, you bastard! I will see you dead…one way or another."

Melanie disconnected the call while her grandfather was still shouting obscenities. The smell of burnt ozone combined with spent black magic filled the air when Jace reached her. Touching her elbow, he had to work hard to keep from smiling when she jumped at his touch. No, it wasn't the time to laugh, but stress does crazy things to people.

"What the hell?" She shrieked, stumbling backward.

Catching her before she hit the pavement, Jace pulled Melanie tight to his chest and spun away from the charred hole in the ground. He'd expected her to pull back or at the very least tense in his arms, so when she curled into him for shelter, his heart swelled with pride. Not willing to let her go, he lifted her into his arms and walked towards her car.

9

Reaching the little red hatchback, Melanie lifted her head and gazed at him through her thick dark lashes. What he saw in the depths of her expressive hazel eyes caused his heart to skip a beat. There were all the amazing characteristics he was already growing to love. But in that moment, he also recognized just a touch of vulnerability coupled with the need for someone she could trust and the spark of affection that Jace prayed would grow into a love to last them a lifetime.

Just as Melanie opened her mouth to speak, a car door slammed behind them and the spell was broken. Before he could take his next breath, she jumped from his arms, turned her back, and pretended to be preoccupied with searching her bag. Embarrassment flooded their link, followed by the telltale blush on her cheeks. Unwilling to let her recriminate herself for simply following the feelings he knew were growing in her heart and soul, Jace gently spun her towards him. She attempted to pull back, but the Guardsman would not be persuaded.

Pushing her out of her comfort zone, he half expected her to swing at him, yell, or at least give him a dirty look, but Melanie was full of surprises. Instead of retaliating, she kept her head bowed and stood motionless. More than a little confused and tired of waiting, Jace slid his thumb under her chin, slowly nudging until they were once again looking into each other's eyes.

Placing his hands on her shoulders, he joked to ease her anxiety. "Rough day at the salt mines?"

Shaking her head, Melanie chuckled. "You could say that. How much of that catastrophe did you see?"

"Would you kick my ass if I said all of it?"

"No, but hiding under the covers for a week or two sounds like a solid plan."

"Want some company?" He waggled his eyebrows and winked.

Swatting him on the shoulder, she retorted, "Yeah, right."

For once in his life, Jace didn't think, he just acted. Slamming his mouth to hers, he demanded immediate entrance. Saying with his kiss what he'd been unable to communicate in any other way. It took only a moment for Melanie to relax against him, opening completely. Her sigh of surrender was music to his ears. Her moans of desire the only encouragement he needed to fall deeper into all that she was.

Jace's hands traveled Melanie's body, loving the feel of her erotic curves and wishing they were somewhere more private where he could strip her naked and enjoy her sensual body with more than his touch. Her hands slid around his neck just as his hands found her ample behind and once again he lifted his mate until only their clothes kept them from becoming one.

Her legs wound around his waist, drowning his denim covered erection in the heat of her desire. They immediately began to move in unison, every meeting of their hips more intense than the last. Melanie mewled into his mouth, her nails dug into the flesh at the base of his neck, and their pace increased until Jace was sure he would lose his mind. His dragon roared, pushing with all his might, driving the Guardsman to claim their mate in every way possible.

Jace's hands slipped under the soft cotton of her scrub top, finally making contact with her bare skin. Sparks flew between them, sending an electric current he was sure could light Times Square on New Year's Eve through his body. The thought of using his enhanced speed entered his lust addled brain at the same time laughter from a passing group of hospital employees sounded to his right and Royce's voice boomed in his mind, *"Get your ass back to the lair. Rayne's called a meeting."*

The older Guardsman's voice in his head was a bucket of water to his libido as he quickly answered, *"Little busy here, old man."*

"Yeah, I caught that. Learn to shield better and getting your rocks off is no excuse. Get. Here. Now."

"Be there as soon as I can," was his quick response as he severed their connection and locked his shields down tight. There was no way he would share one second of his time with Melanie with anyone.

Focusing on the beautiful woman that was scurrying to right her clothing and put as much distance between them as was possible, Jace wanted to scream to the Heavens, "Why me?!" Instead, he spun Melanie around for the second time and met her glare with one of his own, speaking before she had the chance.

"Don't you *dare* try to run and hide from me. I've spent the last four months dreaming of our first real kiss and although this may not have been the way I imagined it, it was absolutely perfect."

He grabbed her by the upper arms as she tried to turn away and forced her to once again meet his eyes. "Talk to me."

"No. Let go of me."

"I will as soon as you talk to me."

"What the hell do you want me to say, Jace? Thank you? It was fun? Let's do it again sometime?"

Jace couldn't stop the bark of laughter that flew from his mouth. Melanie's resulting look would have made a lesser man slink away to lick his wounds, but it only served to fuel his laughter. He watched through watery eyes as she tried to maintain her stance and laughed all the harder when she broke down and laughed along. It wasn't long until they were leaning on one another, barely able to catch their breath.

The first to recover, Jace chuckled, "Well, this night's been a helluva a rollercoaster ride."

"Sure has." She sighed. "I think a beer or four and a soak in a bubble bath is just what I need."

"Wish I could join you." Jace again waggled his eyes, but this time Melanie was quick to cut him off at the pass.

"Hold it right there, Romeo. I was speaking of a solo mission."

"Just as well, I have to get back to the la…home." He quickly corrected, glad she had missed his almost faux pas. Then covered with, "But you can't blame a guy for trying."

"Oh yeah? I'm thinking I've got quite a lot to blame you for." She winked and pulled her keys from her bag.

He loved that she felt comfortable enough to joke with him and hated the fact that he had to leave her, especially after the kiss they'd just shared. Unfortunately, he knew he had maybe two more minutes before Royce or

Heavens forbid Rayne, their Commander, was again yelling in his head.

The beep of her car doors unlocking gave him another sad reminder that he would have to let her go, at least for the time being. Ever the gentleman, Jace reached around his mate, opened the door, and motioned for her to slide into the driver's seat. She gave him a cheeky little grin that he filed away as one of the cutest things he'd ever seen before taking the driver's seat.

Shutting the door, he motioned for her to open the window. Melanie acted as if she were thinking about it, and then chuckled as it slid down. "Yes?" She cooed, batting her eyes and making him once again bark with laughter.

Life with Melanie will never be boring.

"Drive safe. Call me if you need *anything*."

"I'll be fine, Jace."

"Don't argue with me, young lady." He inserted as much authority into his voice as he could without pissing her off, even added a wink and a chuckle for good measure.

"You got it. I'm too tired to argue." She laughed.

"Good. Now get outta here and I'll talk to you tomorrow."

"Aye, aye, Captain." She mock saluted as she started her car.

Jace stepped back and watched her back out and head towards the exit of the parking lot. He waited until the glow of her taillights disappeared into the darkness before heading to his Harley. The ride back to the lair was filled with thoughts of Melanie and the day he would not have to let her go, when she would be by his side *always*.

The sound of Liam's agitation pulled him back to the present. "Dammit, J, tell me what the hell is going on. This is complete and total bullshit."

Jace stopped, let his head fall forward, and blew out a long breath. It was time to come clean or risk losing the one person in the world who'd always been there for him.

Unwilling to face Liam, he began to speak. "I found my mate. It's Melanie…from the hospital."

"Well, duh, no shit."

Jace spun, not believing his ears. "You knew?"

"J, dude, you're not as sneaky as you think you are, never have been and your shielding…well, let's just say you've really gotta work on that."

"Does *everybody* know?"

"Nah, just me, Royce, Devon, and their mates. Everyone else has been so busy with the whole 'Andrew's a traitor, let's kill him. No, he might be okay, let's spare him' thing that they've not been real observant. But what's this impromptu trip to the 'moors' have to do with Nurse Whelan?"

"She's disappeared. Gone without a trace. I searched her condo and found the stench of black magic and followed it here."

"What about the whole mating bond thing I keep hearing about? Can't you find her that way?"

"I tried. I mean, our link's been getting stronger. I've stayed constantly connected to her from the minute I realized she was my destiny, but something changed night before last. Something or someone broke our bond or at the very least interrupted it and is hiding Melanie from me. Her place was a mess, overturned furniture and broken glass everywhere like there'd been a fight. I found a few drops of her blood on the patio and followed the scent into the woods where it disappeared into thin air, just like she has."

His dragon chuffed and blew smoke, incredibly agitated that he had halted their search for even a moment. Jace ignore the beast as Liam answered.

"I should kick your ass on principle alone. Why the hell did you keep that shit to yourself? We've got to get a hold of Rory. He flew back to their lair the other day with Kellan. They can help. Kell may be scary as hell, but he can track like no one I've ever seen."

Jace knew Liam was right. He should've told his friend what was going on but at the time…

The important thing was that every minute Melanie was with her captors was a minute longer they could be hurting her. He could only imagine what she must be going through. Unimaginable retribution was promised to anyone that dared harm even a hair on her head.

After explaining the call he'd overheard from Melanie's grandfather, he added the little bit of information he'd been able to dig up concerning who he believed the man to be. Then Jace took Liam's advice and reached out to Rory, the Commander of the Blue Thunder Force and younger brother to his mentor. *"Rory, I need your help."*

"What's up, young'un? You know I'm back home, right?"

"Yeah," Jace chuckled. *"Me too."*

"Wait. What? You're here? On the shore?"

"Yeah, we're here."

"We?"

"Liam and I."

"Hey, Ror. How's it going?" Liam chimed in.

"Guess I should be asking you boys that."

"Yeah, well, we're tracking someone that's been kidnapped."

"Kidnapped? What the hell? I thought we were over all this shit. Andrew's getting all rehabilitated and everything. We're all one big happy family again. No more drama and all that good stuff. Who in all that's holy has kidnapped who now and for what reason?"

Jace stood silent while Liam filled Rory in on all the details. He pushed with the combined strength of man and beast to locate Melanie through their mating bond but came up empty handed…*again.* Rory's words shocked him out of his quest.

"Son of a bitch! You're sure she called him Grand Draoi?*"*

"Yep, that's what she called him. He also gave a couple shows of his power, but Mel taunted him, said he was losing his strength."

"Wait a minute, she called him seanathair? *They're related?"*

"Yes, sir. I was shocked as you."

"But she's been around us all. I've never felt her magic. I thought she was just an incredibly intelligent, intuitive human."

"No shit! Me too! And I'm her mate!" Jace knew his voice had raised to almost yelling, but the stress of not being able to locate his mate was pushing him past the limits of his control.

"And now that we've all had our moment of shock and awe, we can worry about whether she's magical or not

17

and how she hid it from us later. What do you know about this guy, Rory?" Liam asked and Jace could tell that he too was nearing the end of his rope.

"You remember that coven of black witches and wizards Kyra was talking about, the Dorcha*? Well, their leader is known as the* Grand Draoi, *and he's one seriously messed up bad guy. So if he's who Melanie was talking to, even with waning powers he'd still be able to level cities. It's been said that on his worst day he can literally reach through time and space to rip the soul out of his enemies. Legend states that even though the demon Balor watches over the* Dorcha, *it's Caligrosto that they pray to. And that is one bad ass demon.*

"Caligrosto was spawned from Balor's nightmares that had been marinating in the Dreaming Gulf of the Abyss for literally eons. Can you even imagine what gives a demon god nightmares? Got to be some scary shit. Anyway, ol' Caligrosto demands his followers sacrifice those of their own blood in exchange for power. Which follows what you gathered from Melanie's conversation with her gramps. Are you sure that's who has her?" Jace could hear that Rory was hoping he was mistaken.

"I'm sure. I've either been with this woman or been near her for four months. There have been no other threats, nothing unusual, nada, zip, zilch. Hell, I thought life was gonna be good and boring."

"As if!" Liam and Rory barked in unison.

"Now get your asses over here. I'll rally the troops and we'll be ready to head out as soon as we see you." Rory commanded and then quickly added, *"And Jace…you better let my brother and the others know where you are*

before they come looking. I've never known that lot to just let bygones be bygones, especially if they can torture you."

Jace cringed at the reminder that he was basically AWOL. He answered the only way he could. *"I'll take care of it."*

Closing their connection to the sound of Rory's laughter, the young Guardsman looked at his friend. "Time to get my ass kicked."

CHAPTER TWO

Melanie tested the ropes that held her hands behind her back, trying with all her might to break free. The black bag that had been shoved over her head remained, making it unbearably hot and impossible to see. Sweat covered her face as she fought to not lose her cool while figuring a way out of the fresh hell she found herself in.

Counting to ten, she redirected her focus to her feet, happy to find they were tied together and not to the legs of the chair. She rotated her feet in opposite directions, letting the rope slide over her skin and was happy to find it was good old fashioned jute. Mr. Addison, her high school Chemistry teacher who doubled as the P.E. teacher, would be proud she recognized its texture and even happier that she remembered with enough friction and moisture it would stretch. Ignoring the burning sensation working its way up her legs, she rubbed her ankles against one another as she continued to rotate her feet.

This is like the whole 'rub your tummy and pat your head' game only with my legs and feet. Damn, I'm talented. Now to put everything I've learned from Bruce Willis to work and get the hell outta dodge.

Her muscles ached and threatened to cramp, which only made Melanie work harder. Sweat ran down her legs, soaking the ropes as she listened for the sounds of her captors. It wouldn't do any good to work this hard only to have the rat bastards show up and redo her bindings.

Distracting herself, she thought back to the men that abducted her. It was obvious they'd used black magic. They were from the very Guard she'd taunted her grandfather about. Of course, she full well planned on

smacking herself in the back of the head for letting them
get the jump on her *and* for giving the old wizard the idea.
She'd like to blame her inattention on the conversation with
the *Grand Draoi* and in all truth, it *had* thrown her for a
loop, but it was the mind-blowing kiss from a certain tall,
blue-eyed hunk that had scrambled her neurons and left her
wishing for so much more. She'd been lost to her
daydreaming, allowing the assholes to get the jump on her.
Years and years of honing her skills of observation, always
knowing *everything* that was going on around her, *and*
hiding her magic from even the best mystical practitioners
were skills that kept her safe for almost twenty years.
Melanie had known it was the only shot she would have to
live a normal life, far away from her jacked up family that
put the fun in *dysfunction.*

    Best laid plans...

    The sound of boots striking concrete echoed
through her prison. Stopping cold, Melanie hurried to hide
her escape plans. Doing her best impression of a ragdoll,
she let her body go completely limp and played opossum.
The footsteps grew closer, louder, more pronounced until
she realized that what she'd thought to be one person was
actually two and that the second man had a slight hesitation
every second step. She hoped it meant he had a limp, not
because she wished ill on anyone but because maybe she
could use it to her advantage.

    Doing her best to control her breathing and praying
the approaching goons wouldn't be able to hear the
pounding of her heart, Melanie took one last deep breath,
exhaled...and prayed. Metal scratched against concrete,
followed by a slam, and then the rattle of a heavy chain.

Tumblers of a lock opening completed the scary sonata. Six footsteps later, rough hands grabbed her upper arms, jerking her into a semi-standing position. It took all her concentration and control not to flinch or cry out as pain radiated throughout her arms and shoulders.

Her efforts were rewarded when a low gravelly voice said, "I think you put too much power in your Stunning Spell. It's been almost two days. She should be awake by now. The *Draoi* is gonna be *pissed*. His orders were explicit, she was *not* to be harmed *in any way*," chastised Putz number one.

"Not my fault she's weak. I didn't even go full strength. I can't believe he has us dragging this useless *null* around the countryside. There's *no way* she can be the one of legend." Putz number two grumped.

"Shut the hell up!" Putz one growled. "Do you want the *Draoi* to hear you? The last guy that questioned him ended up as a pile of goo."

Melanie pushed back the bile that had risen at the memory her captor's words revived. She remembered looking on as one of her grandfather's most trusted advisors spoke out against the old wizard's plan du jour. *The* Draoi *had simply raised an eyebrow and the once vital man she'd affectionately called Uncle Jacob for all of her life became a bubbling pea-green puddle of goop. The throne room was completely silent, not one sound from the* Dorcha *in attendance. She wondered for a moment if anyone was breathing.*

Never one to let a chance for drama be wasted, the man that had once upon a time set her upon his shoulders and pretended to be a great stallion began to clap. A slow, staccato slapping of hands that echoed through the round stone room, continually growing in intensity until Melanie, no more than eleven years old at the time, wanted to cower in the corner, covering her ears.

Worse than the applause was the malevolent smile that darkened his face and the gleam of pure evil within his onyx eyes. He stood with all the pomp and circumstance of a true king and strode as if leading a parade to the wet patch that had once been a man. Reaching the edge, he stopped and stared. The bubbling of the goo continued as if chastising the wizard for its existence.

The Grand Draoi *turned to the crowd, raised his arms over his head, and proclaimed, "Let those that agree with our fallen comrade speak now without fear of recrimination. I am, after all, a benevolent ruler."*

Seconds ticked by, it felt as if all the air had been sucked from the room. Melanie squeezed her mother's hand and prayed to be anywhere but there. It seemed like hours had passed when her grandfather finally spoke. His words were something the little girl didn't understood until many years later.

"We each have a role to play. The Dorcha *has not survived for millennia upon millennia without true commitment from each member to follow the path they have been given. Together, we will rule the Earth. Let us all spend the evening in quiet reflection, rededicating ourselves to our one true mission."*

Then the lunatic walked through the puddle of Jacob, humming a show tune as he made his way out of the room, acting like it was all in a day's work. That was the night Melanie's mother had planned their escape.

For weeks after, Joanie Whelan hid money, clothes, and supplies in a hidey hole under the floorboard in their closet. She had a contact outside the coven, who Melanie only knew as Smith. When they escaped, he would be waiting on the other side of the woods to transport them as far away from the Dorcha *as possible.*

The night came when they were to run. Joanie told Melanie to go to After-Dinner Meditation just as always, but instead of returning to their room at its conclusion, she was to meet her mother in the basement and together they would slip away using the underground tunnels.

Everything went as planned for a while. They were running hand-in-hand, following the dim light of the flashlight Joanie had appropriated from the guard's shack when the sound of chanting came from the shadows ahead of them. Within seconds, the low drone of many voices filled the chamber.

"Run, Meli Rose, run," her mother shouted.

She tried, but the dirt beneath her feet had become like quicksand. The harder she pushed, the slower she ran until she fell to her knees sobbing. Somewhere amid all the chanting, running, and fear, Melanie lost contact with Joanie. Trying to stand but only getting as far as her knees, the child swiped at the tears that continued to flow while frantically searching the dark for her mother.

Firm but gentle hands lifted her in the air. Melanie threw back her head and was rewarded with a loud crunch and low moan that could only mean she'd made contact with her jailer's nose. Unfortunately, his grip tightened instead of loosened. It was then she began to kick and flail about. Her efforts were rewarded when the heel of the climbing boots her mother had demanded she wear made contact with his crotch.

Her captor howled like a wounded dog and dropped her on the ground. Melanie sprinted into the darkness, praying to whoever was listening that she be reunited with her mom. Instead, she was scooped up and immediately bound and gagged before being carried right back to the man she never wanted to see again.

"Tsk, tsk, tsk, Meli Rose. Where exactly did you think you could go that I can't find you?"

She opened her mouth to tell him to go to hell, even though she was sure her mom would wash her mouth out with soap, when the scrape of the large door at the rear of the room drew her attention. In walked six of her grandfather's guard carrying Joanie atop their shoulders. She was trussed up like a calf at a rodeo and seemed to be under the influence of a Paralyzing Spell. Her eyes were wide but unseeing, her mouth open in a silent scream, and her body stiff as a board.

"Mom!" Melanie called over and over until her screams were little more than a whisper, but Joanie never so much as moved. Dried tears stained her cheeks, though she hadn't realized she was crying.

Sarah Beth, one of her mother's best friends, knelt before her and pulled Melanie into her embrace, rocking and assuring her everything would be okay. The older woman whispered for only her to hear. "Please calm yourself, child. Don't make matters worse for you or your mother. Do your best to be strong and pray Joanie can get herself out of this mess."

One look at her grandfather told her the kind witch was right. Summoning a strength much older than her years, Melanie stopped crying, stood, and waited like the good little Dorcha *she was supposed to be while everything in her was shouting that she unleash her power on everyone in sight. Her magic was all she had left. It was the one secret she'd been able to keep, even from her mom.*

Melanie Rose Whelan was more naturally magical than anyone in their coven had been for over a thousand years. It wasn't something she'd wished for or even knew she possessed until *the eve of her tenth birthday. On that night she was visited by the Goddess Anu, the keeper of magic. The goddess explained that Melanie's father, who died when she was a baby, had given his life in an attempt to bring light to the* Dorcha. *It was now her job to continue his quest. Anu went on to explain that Cleland, Melanie's grandfather and the* Draoi, *was quickly perfecting his ability to call and control demons. She warned that if he were allowed to continue, no* one *would be safe. The world as they knew it would cease to exist. Her parting words were something Melanie had worked hard for years to forget.*

"You possess the power, Melanie Rose Whelan. You and you alone can stop him. One day you will be called upon. Do not let us down."

Movement brought Melanie back to the present, just in time to hear the captor she referred to as Putz Two say, "Why can't we just leave her here? Send the others after her? The *Grand Draoi* will never know, and if anything happens to her, it'll be on them."

Well, this one's not the brains of the operation.

"Because, dumbass, the *Draoi* asked us *personally* to bring his granddaughter back into the fold. Remember? This is our mission and one we *cannot* fuck up." It was obvious Putz One was at the end of his rope with his cohort but stuck with him nonetheless.

"Oh, yeah. Well, dammit. Then we better get the bitch awake."

Melanie thought about pulling out her magic and dusting it off when he called her a bitch. Then changed her mind. It would be more beneficial for her to remain quiet and listen. She only needed to wait for the right time and then she could make the asshole's balls fall off.

It wasn't long before the idiots gave up and left the room. She heard them discussing different ways they could get her awake without harm and even what to do with her body if she never woke. A cellphone rang during their conversation. Putz One answered and began stammering, quickly explaining their plight. Apparently, whoever was on the other end of the phone had more common sense than her two captors combined, because when they returned, the idiots made short work of her bindings, removed the hood from her head, and carried her into what she could smell from the disinfectant was the bathroom.

Melanie was unceremoniously dumped on a cold tile floor and barely avoided banging her head against the wall while maintaining her ruse. However, she wasn't as lucky when the icy spray of a shower hit her square in the face. Unable to feign unconsciousness while drowning in ice cubes, she gasped and tried to catch her breath. Scrambling backward in a crab walk, she tried to climb out of the tub to avoid what felt like hail against her skin.

Son of a bitches had to grab me when I was in a tank top and boxers. Couldn't have gotten me a sweatshirt and jeans?

"Lookie there, the princess is awake."

Throwing her best 'die bastard' look at her kidnappers, Melanie spat, "I'm awake, assholes. Turn the damn water off."

Pushing her soggy bangs from her eyes, she focused on the Putz Twins, not surprised that they looked like all the other men her *seanathair* had appointed to his guard, big and dumb. The good news was that it seemed the leader of the *Dorcha* hadn't changed much. He still did things the same way and that was something she could use to her advantage. The bad news was he picked huge, muscle bound wizards who used their fists to make up for what they lacked in magical ability. From the look of the two that stood staring at her like she was an exhibit at the county fair, they were no exception. She knew Putz Two had stunned her but figured that was the height of his talent…or at least she hoped it was.

After a few tense moments, the bald one threw a towel at her and commanded, "Dry off, cover up, and stand up."

She recognized his voice as belonging to Putz One, the more intelligent of the two, not that either one was up for admission into Mensa, but it helped her to know who was who. Melanie did as she was told and was soon being dragged back to her chair. Putz Two knelt before her and made quick work of tying her ankles to the legs of the chair this time with leather straps. Putz One wrapped the same straps, only wider, around her midsection, securing her left arm to her side as he went. She wanted to chuckle. Apparently Cleland remembered she was left-handed and thought that securing her dominant hand would keep her from using magic. Little did **he** know that had nothing to do with her refusal to call upon her gifts.

After incapacitating her right hand the same way he had her left, Putz One spoke. "Let's go. We need to report in."

An acknowledging grunt from Putz Two and they walked out the door without another word. The sound of the chain and lock being secured on the other side of the door followed by their retreating footsteps was the last thing Melanie heard for almost two hours. She laughed to herself at how good she was at telling time without a watch. It was a skill she had mastered during her nurse's training. Because of the magic that ran through her veins, even though suppressed by the charm of Cerridwen, she couldn't wear a watch. Well, she could wear one but after a few hours of contact with her skin, the timepiece would simply cease to function, never to keep time again. It happened with every type of timepiece she tried, even a pocket watch that had been her father's. In order to not spend her life late for *everything*, she'd been forced to learn to keep time in her head.

Thinking about all the crazy things that had happened in her almost twenty-nine years was a mixed bag of emotions, but she had to admit there was more good than bad, especially lately. She smiled to herself when the image of spiky blond hair and mischievous blue eyes popped into her head. Other parts of her tingled when she thought of the amazing kiss they'd shared right before her abduction. Jace

MacQuaid *definitely* topped the list of positive things in her life.

When he'd first popped into her life, she'd been suspicious. It had been years since anyone had come looking for her, but she still had to be cautious. The thought of using her hidden magic had crossed her mind several times but just the thought of being forced to live among the *Drocha* again stilled her actions. Instead, she had waited and watched, all the while trying to come up with a plausible answer for the immediate attraction she felt for him.

About a week into what she laughingly called her 'surveillance', Melanie noticed Jace watching her. It hadn't taken long until their occasional smiles turned to 'hellos', which turned to a quick 'how's your day' now and then, to cups of coffee on her breaks, lunches together, and then long talks in the parking lot after work. She realized early on what a truly nice guy he was, and now she had the memory of their first *real* kiss to keep her from losing her mind while in captivity.

The longer she thought of Jace, the stronger the feeling that he was thinking about her became. It was as if she could actually *feel* his thoughts and emotions. She knew they were supposed to talk the day after their kiss and figured he thought she'd blown him off, but for some reason, that didn't fit what she knew of the man. Closing her eyes, Melanie focused on the warmth she felt around her heart at just the thought of his name. She pictured the six-foot-three-inch man that scrambled her brains with his cocky grin and genuine heart and felt an immediate sense of relief. No matter how impossible it sounded, even in her own head, she *knew* he was looking for her.

Her heart beat faster as she tried to think of a way to contact him. It had been almost seventeen years since she'd used her magic. The day she ran away from the coven, she'd locked all her abilities away with an ancient spell Sarah Beth had given her. From that moment forward, she'd lived her life as a *null* and believed she was better for it. There was a trap door woven into the spell that would allow her to unlock her powers by uttering a simple phrase and removing the charm, but of course that would also allow any magical being she came in contact with to identify her as a witch. It would also signal the *Draoi* of her true power, something she knew he would kill everyone in his path to possess.

Debating whether to reveal herself or trust in the man that was quickly becoming an integral part of her life to find her, Melanie almost jumped out of her skin when she heard the sound of the chains outside her cell rattling. Preparing for what she was sure to be a whopping good time with the Putz Brothers, she was shocked to see a young woman, with long strawberry blonde curls, wearing a light blue T-shirt and jeans enter the room.

The newcomer was carrying a tray of food and an overnight bag. With her head bowed, her beautiful locks covered her face, but that didn't hide the familiarity Melanie felt from the stranger. Stepping just inside the door, she turned just as Putz One snarled, "The *Draoi* said you have one hour. I'll be back to get you. Be waiting at this door. No exceptions."

Melanie wanted to scream for him to go to hell but instead focused on her visitor, who remained facing the door until it was once again secured. As she turned, the young woman lifted her head. A past long forgotten came rushing back. It was Hannah, Sarah Beth's youngest daughter and Melanie's best friend growing up.

"Oh my goddess, Hannah, you're a sight for sore eyes!"

Rushing towards her, Hannah carefully placed the tray she carried on the small table at the side of the bed and dropped the duffle bag before enveloping Melanie in a big warm hug. Unable to embrace her back, Melanie burrowed her head against Hannah's shoulder, soaking in the comfort her friend offered.

After several long minutes, the younger woman slowly released Melanie and leaned back until she was kneeling before her. Still smiling the same sweet smile Melanie remembered from all those years ago, Hannah looked her over from head to toe, shaking her head and tsk'ing as she went. Bending down, she began untying the restraints on Melanie's left ankle.

"Those morons are gonna be crow chow when the *Draoi* sees how they treated you." Hannah sighed without looking up.

When she had both Melanie's ankles free, Hannah began on the leather strapped across her arm and torso while she chatted on about her mom and sisters. Melanie listened intently, glad to hear no one had ever figured out it was Sarah Beth and her family that had aided with her escape. She tried to think of something witty to say, but for the first time in her life, Melanie was speechless.

How do I make up for leaving her in that hellhole all those years ago?

"When mom heard a rumor you'd been found, we all prayed it wasn't true, but here you are." Hannah shook her head as if somehow that would change the situation then continued. "All **the** girls you might've known from your time at the coven were called together. The *An Dara* asked for a volunteer to get you ready for your audience with the *Grand Draoi*. Damon, who became Cleland's second a few years ago, remembered you and I had been close and picked me right away."

Pulling the last leather strap from Melanie's arm, Hannah stood and grinned. "Okay, troublemaker, you're free now. Well, as free as you can get locked away in the basement of an abandoned warehouse."

Melanie sprang from the chair, grabbing her old friend and holding on for dear life. It was the closest she'd felt to sane in the last two days. Only Hannah's laughing made Melanie loosen her grip and step back, but she kept contact by holding her hands. She knew it was silly, but deep down inside she just knew if she let go, Hannah would disappear.

Always incredibly intuitive, Hannah smiled a sweet smile, squeezed her hands, and winked. "I'm not going anywhere, Meli Rose. We have an hour to get you fed and clothed."

The smell of food along with Hannah's reassurances had Melanie letting go of her friend's hands and heading for the table. Her stomach growled and both girls laughed out loud as she lifted the cover off her meal.

"No way! Fiona's still managing the kitchen?" Melanie giggled like a little girl as she stared at what had been one of her favorite meals when she was a kid, tomato soup with homemade croutons, grilled cheese, and fresh strawberry pie. "Your sister always made sure I had this exact meal for my birthday, any time she'd heard about me getting in trouble, or when I needed cheering up."

I guess knowing I'm about to be sacrificed by my grandfather so he can take over the world counts as a time I need cheering up.

Both ladies chuckled as Melanie sat down to eat and Hannah unpacked the overnight bag. "I'm glad to see we're still close to the same size. Hurry up and eat so you can get a shower before Henry and Simon come back. If you haven't noticed, they're not the brightest bulbs in the pack. This is their last chance to complete a mission without screwing it up or the *Draoi* promised to turn them into white mice and feed them to his pet snake."

They have names. Who knew?

Melanie shivered remembering the thirteen-foot, hundred-pound, red-skinned boa constrictor that accompanied her *seanathair* everywhere. It didn't matter they barely had a brain between them, had kidnapped her, and let us not forget called her a bitch, she really didn't want to watch while Diablo ate them. Speaking of eating, her food was getting cold and nothing, not even the thought of Cleland and his snake, was going to keep her from enjoying her meal.

Hannah chatted away about all that had happened while Melanie had been away. Listening intently, it was obvious things were still status quo at the coven. She was glad to hear five of Hannah's six sisters were healthy and well. Sad to know Mara had disappeared after a weird meeting with the *Draoi.* Melanie laughed when her friend told how Sarah Beth kept trying to marry them all off while they, in turn, scared all would be suitors away by any means necessary.

Swallowing her last bite, Melanie jumped up, grabbed the fresh towel Hannah had unpacked, and headed for the shower. Fifteen minutes later she was clean, dressed, and sitting cross-legged on the bed, wondering what was next. Thankfully, she didn't have to wait long. Hannah sat across from her and leaned in, motioning for Melanie to follow suit. When they were bent at the waist, foreheads almost touching, Hannah started whispering.

"In about ten minutes the boys will be back to get us. I'm sorry, but I have to tie you to that damned chair again. I don't want one of those idiots to come in and see you free. They will freak out. If you didn't notice, they're not the best wizards in the coven. Goddess knows you might end up with three heads or worse yet, exploded all over the walls." She shuddered and Melanie had to wonder how many people the ding-dong duo had already blown up.

"Anyway," Hannah continued, "Damon told me to render you unconscious and paralyzed for the trip back, so you're gonna need to give an Oscar winning performance before they put that stupid hood over your head again. Neither one of them will realize I've changed a word or two. You will only sleep for a few minutes and no way would I ever leave you immobile. They're going to take us to a train that will transport us to the coven. Hopefully, Mom and the others will have figured out a way to get you off that train. If not, we'll figure out something once we're back at *Ghealach Dearg*. We have three nights until the blood moon."

Melanie tried to share in Hannah's optimism but had to wonder what the odds were on escaping fate twice in one lifetime. Thoughts of what it had been like to be under Cleland's control all those years ago made her sick with fear, not only for herself but for those she knew would give their lives to help her.

Just about to share her thoughts with Hannah, images of Jace bombarded her consciousness. It was as if she was watching him through the lens of a camera. He was walking through a wooded area with a group of the largest men she'd ever seen. They looked like the men from the hospital that Jace called *brethren,* but she didn't recognize any of their faces. Jace looked sad but determined. She *knew* he was thinking of her. It gave her the hope she needed to finally answer Hannah.

"We just have to make sure no one gets hurt and Cleland never finds out that any of you helped me. You have to promise me, Hannah, and make your mom and sisters promise, as well. *No one* gets hurt on my account."

Melanie held out her fist with her pinkie standing at attention, just like they had as children. The big difference was, they were witches and when witches pinkie swore while calling upon Britania, the goddess of the moon, that pinkie promise became binding. Hannah shook her head, wrapped her pinkie finger around Melanie's, and muttered, "Mom's gonna kill me."

No sooner had they made their promise than the chains outside her door rattled. Melanie dove for the chair.

Hannah whispered a spell and within two heartbeats, Melanie's bindings were just as they had been when Hannah had entered the room.

Her old friend winked and mouthed, *"Showtime,"* right before Melanie's world went black.

CHAPTER THREE

Jace had now experienced something far more scary than Kellan Aherne…and without a scar or brooding onyx eyes. Royce when he was truly pissed! Jace couldn't remember a time in his life that he'd been so thoroughly chewed out, not even when he'd broken the steeple of the chapel during his first attempt at flight. The ass chewing he received from the older Guardsman was epic and both clans had witnessed every bloody word of it.

When he and Liam had arrived at the lair of the Blue Dragons, Rory had been waiting with Kellan and the rest of their Force. All six of them were packed and ready for a briefing, but just as Jace had started to speak, Rory's cellphone rang. One look at the display and the phone was unceremoniously handed to Jace.

Not thinking and without looking, he slid his finger across the screen and answered. A mistake, by the way, he would never make again. Royce's voice boomed through the receiver with such force that Jace had to hold it as far away from his ear as his arm would reach and it still echoed through his skull. The older Guardsman's tirade went on and on. Jace couldn't get a word in edgewise and the worst part was the knowing grins on all the Guardsmen's faces. It was utterly humiliating and something he *had* to endure because after all, he was wrong and busted dead to rights.

His ass-chewing continued for almost thirty minutes and only ended when Devon, the calmest of their Force, took the phone from Royce.

"Do you have any leads?" The Guardsman they all called the Zen Master asked.

"I can tell I'm getting close, but something is keeping me from using our mating link. I've tried everything I know of but other than old fashioned tracking, I've come up empty-handed."

"Look, Jace, I know what you're going through but don't give up. Royce, Kyra, Lance, and I will be there by morning."

The young Guardsman couldn't stop the groan that crossed his lips and wished it back when Devon snickered. "Don't worry, young'un, the old man will be cooled off by then. If he isn't, I'll remind him what he's like when Kyra is out of his sight."

Everyone, including the men standing behind him, chuckled. "Thanks, Dev. I know what I did was wrong but…" He paused trying to find the right words.

Thankfully, Devon finished the sentence for him. "But she's your mate and nothing matters as much as finding her."

Jace nodded. "Yeah, that about sums it up."

"Don't worry. We'll find her. You're with the best tracker I've ever seen and on his home turf."

"Thanks, Dev."

"You're welcome. Now give the phone to Rory, Royce needs to talk to him."

Handing the phone back to his mentor's younger brother, Jace asked Brannoc if there was a place he and Liam could get something to eat and take a quick shower. They were directed to the dorms where the trainees from other clans stayed during their training. After a quick shower and fresh clothes, both young Guardsmen felt themselves again but they were still starving. It only took a few minutes to locate the kitchen, empty the refrigerator, and make two huge sandwiches.

They ate until they were full, cleaned up their mess, and were heading out the door when two of the Guardsmen Jace didn't know, that had been standing with Rory, came walking into the room.

"I'm Declan and this is Pearce." The taller of the two announced as he made his way to the refrigerator and grabbed two bottles of water. Tossing one to his friend, he leaned against the counter and took a long drink from his bottle.

"Nice to meet you." Jace and Liam answered in unison, making the other Guardsmen grin.

"Rory's still on the phone with Royce and Kyra. Seems the little witch knows of the *Dorcha* and wants to check her facts before they head over here and we go hunting."

"Great," was the only response Jace could muster. Just the thought of having a face-to-face 'discussion' with Royce made him wish for a magic spell to turn back time. Unfortunately, he was going to have to suck it up and take his lumps.

Declan laughed out loud. "Don't sweat it young'un, Royce is all bluster. We all grew up with him. He and Rian used to make all our lives miserable. Rian would set us up with his practical jokes and Roy would kick our asses when we fell for it. Just nod your heads and say 'yes, sir' while he bitches and it'll be over before you know it."

"Hell, that little witch mate of his might even have him calmed down by the time they get here. She's a keeper, ya know. Best thing that ever happened to the old man."

Pearce spoke for the first time and Jace decided he liked him already.

They all stood around talking until Rory's voice sounded in their minds. *"Head 'em up. Move 'em out. Meet us in the Ancestor's Hall."*

Jace and Liam followed the other Guardsmen across the training pitch, past a few smaller buildings to an ivy-covered building. Six stone columns stood guard around the porch that led to a set of huge black double doors with brass doorknockers the shape of dragon's heads. As Jace came closer to the pillars, he recognized the story of the dragon shifter's existence carved into the stone in the glyphs that made up the language of the first dragons. It confirmed what he'd always been told, that the story was an integral part of every lair.

Pearce and Declan opened the doors, motioning for him and Liam to enter the hall. Standing at the head of a large oak table that bore the crest of their clan, carved in intricate detail, was Rory with the same shit-eating grin Jace was beginning to think the older Guardsman had been born with. The other Guardsmen were seated around the table, chatting among themselves.

As Rory spoke the others became silent. "Now that we're all here, let's recap a bit so we can get this show on the road." Looking directly at Jace he added, "Tell us what you know and then I'll fill in the gaps with what Kyra just told me about the *Dorcha*."

Jace looked to Liam for help, but the grin on his friend's face made it clear…Jace was on his own. Taking a deep breath, he recounted Melanie's conversation with her grandfather, told how their mating bond had grown stronger then suddenly disappeared. He finished with the scene he found at her home. No one spoke, but he saw the look of concentration on every Guardsman's face. Waiting as patiently as possible, he started to count, a trick he'd learned from his father.

"Counting chickens, bro?" Liam's voice sounded in his mind.

"No dumbass, just trying to keep my cool."

"And how's that working for ya?"

"Not so great. What if…"

"Now stop that shit right there, J. There's no way any of us is gonna let anything happen to your mate." Liam cut him off, speaking with an authority Jace rarely heard from his laid back friend.

"Damn straight," Rory added, catching them both off guard. Chuckling, he continued, *"You guys suck at shielding."*

"Yeah, you really do." Everyone in the room laughed.

Kellan was the first to speak out loud, his Scottish brogue so prevalent it took Jace's brain a minute to translate. "Do you have anything of lass' with you? Anything from her home that her kidnappers may have touched?"

Grabbing his backpack, Jace pulled out the scrub top Melanie had been wearing the last time he saw her, as well as her keys and a few pieces of a broken knickknack he'd found on her bedroom floor. Handing them to Kellan as if they were the most precious treasures in the world, Jace prayed they would help with their search.

The scarred Guardsman placed the items on the table, closed his eyes, and seemed to be centering himself. Jace watched as he slowly opened his eyes, carefully picked up the largest shard of the broken collectible and focused. It was so unexpected, it made the younger Guardsman want to ask what was going on but could see from the solemn expressions around the table that his questions would not be welcome.

Time marched on and on. Impatient, Jace continued to reach through the silent mating bond, searching for any sign of his mate. His frustration grew when again he emerged empty handed. The thought of pacing to burn off some of his nervous energy crossed his mind at the same time Liam spoke through their unique mindspeak link, which thankfully ensured privacy. *"Chill J, Kellan's the best. Just give him a few more minutes. From the looks of it, he's almost done."*

"Damn, I hope you're right."

The words had no sooner left his mouth than Kellan began speaking. "Your mate was one of the *Dorcha* but that was long ago. It appears she renounced her affiliation, which is a real feat considering she's a member of their 'royal family'. She also hid away her magic at a very young age and has had no contact with anything magical, except us, since that time. Her kidnappers were male, doused in black magic, and most definitely part of the *Dorcha*."

Kellan paused. Jace braced himself, afraid to breathe until the retired marine started again. "She's in a room in what appears to be a warehouse or an abandoned industrial facility of some type. The wizards must be sure they've gotten away with her abduction because they have no camouflage – magical or otherwise – on the building, only an Isolation Spell on her. She's deep within its walls, but we can find her."

The Guardsman relaxed against the back of his chair, took a deep breath, and looked around the room. His brethren nodded their appreciation while absorbing what he'd said. Kellan's skills were legendary, but Jace had never expected them to be so detailed and … *mystical*. No one else seemed surprised. They were preparing to follow the war hero anywhere he led.

"Kellan will lead. Brannoc, you and your maps are second. Pearce, Declan, Jace, and Liam spread out in the middle. Lennox and I will bring up the rear. I'd hate for the mad bomber here to blow anyone up." He chuckled at his own joke as Lennox shrugged like it might actually happen, then Rory added, "Mac will meet us if he makes it back in time."

"Mac?" Jace asked.

"Yeah, he's the weapons expert of the Force. Something happened at his ancestral homelands that required his attention a few weeks ago. I told him what was going on as soon as you got here. He said he'd do his best to make it back but not to wait." Declan explained. "His exact words were actually, 'Find that boy's mate'."

The room erupted in laughter and Jace took his first deep breath since walking through those enormous double doors. He hadn't realized how nervous he really was that they wouldn't find Melanie until just that moment. A thought that chilled both man and beast to their core.

In less than ten minutes all eight Guardsmen were loaded into two black SUVs heading in the direction Kellan had indicated. There was no conversation, just a buzz indicating they were all deep in thought as they made the sixty minute drive. The closer they got to the location, the harder Jace prayed.

We will find her. We have to find her.

Not wanting to alert any of the *Dorcha* that might be hidden and guarding the facility, it was decided they'd park a few miles away then hike through the dilapidated industrial park to the rear of the building. As soon as the parking garage Brannoc had indicated on one of his old maps came into view, the Guardsmen gathered their packs, preparing to exit the vehicles.

Jace was in awe of the incredible focus and dedication he felt coming from each man. It wasn't anything he hadn't seen with his own clan, but in this case, it was *all* for him and Melanie. He knew he should thank them, but as he started to speak, Rory tapped his temple, indicating they were to use mindspeak and only if absolutely necessary. The one thing about black magic that none of them, including Kyra, had been able to figure out was when or if a dark magic practitioner could sense the dragons' mindspeak, so they had to be careful.

Taking formation, they set out into the dark night using their enhanced vision. The first two miles of their trek was uneventful, which should've eased Jace's tension but instead made him more nervous. Without something to keep his mind busy, he thought of Melanie and what she must be going through. His dragon chuffed and blew smoke, pushing the man to let him out. It was tempting, but the young Guardsman had already caused enough trouble and decided he liked breathing.

Royce would kill me and then have Kyra bring me back just so he could do it again.

Chuckling at his own joke, Jace ran straight into Pearce's back as Royce's voice sounded in his mind. *"What exactly am I kicking your ass for this time?"*

"Nothing. Nothing at all," Jace hurriedly answered while mouthing his apology to Pearce, who just shrugged it off and kept moving forward.

"Yeah, yeah, yeah. I've heard that before."

"Give the kid a break, Roy. He's stressed about his girl." Rory interjected, saving Jace from anymore chastising from his mentor.

"See you in ten." Royce growled and cut their connection.

Thankful for Rory's intervention, Jace turned his attention back to tracking. He knew Kellan was older and better at it, but there was no way the younger Guardsman was going to let anyone else get to *his* mate first. He would do everything possible to have his face be the first she saw when she was rescued.

True to his words, in exactly ten minutes Royce, Kyra, Devon, Lance, and a fifth figure Jace didn't immediately recognize appeared over the last small ridge, standing between the search party and the abandoned industrial park. As they closed the distance, the young Guardsman recognized the sleek figure as Maxmillian Prentisse aka Max, the King of the Big Cats. It was a welcome surprise. The werepanther could get into places man nor dragon could, was a hell of a tracker in his own right, and could fight with the best of them. None of which the dragons liked to admit but all did in the name of cohabitation of the species.

There was no discussion, just a look between brothers and the two groups became one, traversing the remaining landscape in record time. No dark witches or wizards could be seen. Every Guardsman reached out with his enhanced senses but again came up empty-handed.

Rory momentarily broke their silence. *"Anybody getting anything inside or out?"*

"No," was the general consensus.

"I can't get a read past the ground level. It's like everything lower is covered in a fog," Devon added. Not good news considering the older Guardsman was one of the strongest in mental ability Jace had ever met.

"All right, teams of three, Kyra with Roy, fan out just as we planned. Jace, you go with Kellan and Declan to the room your Melanie is in. She'll need a friendly face," Rory commanded.

"Yes, sir," Jace answered as he moved into position.

"Did you hit your head, kid?" Lance asked.

"No, sir, why?"

"I haven't heard this many 'yes, sir's' or witnessed this much butt kissing since you let the horses out when you were a teenager." Lance laughed out loud at his own joke while Jace shook his head and the rest of the dragons ignored the jokester.

Just another reminder of why his nickname is 'pain in the ass'.

Focusing on Kellan's movements, careful to follow all his hand signals, Jace opened his senses as wide as he could and searched for Melanie. Their slow, methodical descent into the basement was nerve wracking. All he and his dragon could think of was how long their mate had already been in the clutches of the mad leader of a crazy black magic coven.

When they came up empty-handed, Jace's beast roared in his head, chuffing and blowing smoke, demanding to be let out. Using all the control he'd been taught, he finally calmed his dragon and a few deep breaths later was calm again himself.

Kellan directed them to a set of hidden stairs leading to the sub-basement. Again, they followed the same procedure. Stepping onto the lowest level of the building, Melanie's scent flooded Jace's senses. Not wanting to break rank but finding it hard to remain calm, he called to Kellan.

"She's here. I can scent her."

"Me, too, but she's not alone, if she's there at all. I sense at least two males and another female, all doused in black magic. Rory says take anyone we find alive so we have a chance to interrogate and find the whole coven. That means we need to approach from two sides and as carefully as possible."

"What do you mean if she's there at all?"

"Exactly what I said. Can you get a good read on anything but her scent?"

Jace wanted to argue but knew it wouldn't do any good. He had to admit Kellan was right. He wanted Melanie back as quickly as possible, so he took his hundredth deep breath and fell back in line. They reached a fork in the hallway. Declan signaled he was taking the left and pointed for Jace to follow Kellan to the right.

Just like they had on the last level, they looked around every corner, behind every door, and inside every nook and cranny, carefully working their way to the room they both identified as Melanie's prison. They turned the last corner and met Declan coming towards them. He pointed at the only door they hadn't gone through. The door that was keeping him from his mate. Unfortunately, instead of looking forward to seeing her beautiful smile, Jace's heart fell and his dragon snarled at the sight before them. The door was ajar, a chain had been haphazardly hung over an enormous hinge lock that from the shine of the metal had only been attached a few days earlier and there was a massive padlock hung through one of the links.

Stepping around Kellan with the full intent of rushing into the room, Jace was stopped midstride by the older Guardsman's hand on his shoulder.

"Move that hand or lose it." Jace growled.

Doing just the opposite and gripping even tighter, Kellan returned his growl with one of his own. *"Stop and think. If she's in there, you don't need to see her. Let us look first. What's more likely is that they've already moved her and the room is booby trapped. Again, something we're better prepared to handle."*

As much as he hated to admit it, Jace had to agree. He was ninety-nine percent sure Melanie was not in that room. He had let her down again. Hadn't gotten here in time. To say he was pissed was an understatement. Kellan's voice pulled him out of his pity party.

*"Pull your head outta your ass. We need to secure
that room and get in there before the trail goes cold."*

Without another word, Kellan nodded towards
Declan and in unison they moved towards the door with
Jace in tow. In less than two minutes, the three of them had
entered the room, found no magical traps, and were
searching for clues. Thankfully, Melanie's kidnappers had
been sloppy. A tray of half eaten food was left on the bed,
the clothes he guessed she'd been wearing when they
abducted her were thrown in a pile on the bathroom floor,
along with a damp towel. There was also a hairbrush he
was sure she'd used sitting on the back of the sink.

Gathering all the evidence, Jace returned to the
main room and took a moment to look at the straight back
wooden chair and leather restraints he knew without a
doubt had immobilized his mate. Fury like he'd never felt
filled his entire being and that of his dragon. The longer he
stared, the more irate they became. He imagined Melanie's
soft creamy skin abraded with the rough leather straps and
promised slow, treacherous retribution to any and all that
had dared touch her.

Needing to be anywhere but in that room, Jace
headed for the door. No longer needing to use only
mindspeak, he yelled over his shoulder, "I need some air.
See you outside."

Not waiting for an answer, he sped towards the
stairs. Taking them two at a time, he hit the floor of the
basement just as Kyra and Royce were heading down.

"Kellan wants Kyra to take a look at the room
where Melanie was." He heard Royce say as he passed and
threw a grunt of acknowledgement over his shoulder. Jace

knew he'd need to apologize later but was not about to stop his assent.

Jogging across the basement floor, he finally reached the stairs leading to the ground level and the blessed fresh air he so badly needed. This time he took the stairs three at a time, thinking of nothing else but tearing Melanie's kidnappers limb from limb. He was so engrossed in his plotting he barely heard the whisper of a voice fighting for his attention.

"Jace…"

Stopping dead in his tracks and thanking the Heavens for the enhanced senses that kept him from rolling down the steps he's just climbed, Jace listened. It seemed to take forever but finally he heard it again, just slightly louder than before.

"If you really are looking for me, and my heart says you are, look for the Blackthorn trees with the blood red blossoms. They only grow near the coven. Jace, I wanted…" Her voice trailed off and Jace felt the connection break.

Running as fast as he could, retracing his steps and bellowing for all his brethren to hear, Jace announced, "Blackthorn **trees**! We need to find the damn Blackthorn trees!"

CHAPTER FOUR

Melanie had no idea if Jace heard what she was saying. If she was being honest, she had no idea why she believed he would, she just did. The overwhelming feeling in her heart and soul that he was out there looking for her and they were linked…*bonded* in some way, kept her going and made her reach out to him. Being hidden away deep in the bowels of the coven she'd fled all those years ago made her hope for the improbable and pray for the impossible. If there was any way she was going to survive, it was going to take everything she could come up with and a few things she'd just have to pull out of her ass at the right time.

She was glad Hannah had knocked her out before her captors had entered the room. At least she was spared listening to them on the trip back to the coven. When she woke up, it was as if she'd been transported back in time. Her surroundings so familiar that she closed and opened her eyes several times, praying what she saw was a dream. Unfortunately, it was all too real.

Groaning, Melanie rolled on her stomach, buried her head in the fluffy pink covered pillows, and screamed as long and as loud as she could. That stupid asshole, aka the *Grand Draoi,* and more importantly, aka her *grandfather* (only by genetics) had plopped her right back in the room from her childhood. She figured the deluded leader of the *Dorcha* thought he was doing her a big favor. That she should somehow see it as how much he loved her that he'd kept her room just as it had been all those years ago. Truth was, it made her sick. She actually wanted to throw up at the thought of him keeping all her things like some shrine to her existence when in actuality, he just wanted to kill her and steal her powers.

I know all families have their issues, but not even Dr. Phil's got an answer for this shit!

The only difference between the past and the present was the new clothes hanging in the antique wardrobe and the white silk ceremonial robe that made her skin crawl. The asshole really had some nerve. Hanging a 'death shroud' next to plain, old, every day clothing like it was a foregone conclusion that she would march to her own death without raising seven kinds of hell and taking as many of the ass kissing *Drocha* with her as she could.

Finally climbing out of the giant four poster bed, she padded into the bathroom, washed her face and returned, then decided to see exactly how bad things really were. She turned the door knob, not surprised to find it locked and even less shocked to hear a guard outside her door. Next, she checked all four windows, laughing at the iron bars and wondering who the old man had gotten to install them since iron was a witch's kryptonite. She hoped it was Putz One and Two.

Lastly, she went to the vent inside the linen closet just outside the bathroom door. It had been her escape hatch more times than she could count, especially after her mother's untimely demise. Melanie was thrilled to see they hadn't found it and completely pissed when she realized how much bigger adult Melanie was than twelve year old Melanie. Her head and shoulders fit through the opening but that was where the buck stopped. Her ample bosom that most of the time she thought was pretty cool became nothing but a hindrance as she tried to squeeze into the shaft.

Sweating and exasperated, she backed out of the vent, collapsed on to the floor, and pouted. It was defeating, to say the least, for Melanie to admit that she was trapped in a room she'd hoped to never see again, in a place she'd never wanted to visit again, about to be confronted by a man she'd hoped would die before he caught up to her. Of course, none of that mattered, she had to find a way out. There was no way she could let Sarah Beth, Hannah, or any of the other people that had been friends of her mother help her escape. Yes, they had all done it before and not been found out, but letting them do it again would tempt Fate in the worst way.

And let's face it, Fate has NOT been good to me lately.

Then she thought of Jace and had to admit that someone up there was looking out for her. She thought about the crazy ESP message she'd sent him and wondered for the tenth time if he *really* was looking for her. No sooner had the thought crossed her mind than the little voice she'd always depended on to get her through the hard times whispered, *"He is. And he's bringing reinforcements."*

She laughed out loud and shook her head, wondering when she'd lost her marbles. But she'd learned early in her career as a nurse that hope was all people needed to believe and if they believed, they could accomplish damn near anything. If there was anyone that could accomplish saving her from the mess she was sitting smack in the middle of, it was the amazing man that had captured her eye and was working on her heart.

Sitting in the bathroom, contemplating life as she knew it, the main door to her room swung open and in rushed Hannah. Her cheeks were flushed and she was out of breath as she balanced a tray of food in one hand and a pitcher of tea in the other while trying to kick the door shut.

Melanie jumped up and ran to help. "What the hell? You can't even help with the damn door?" She shouted at the guard as the door clicked shut.

Grabbing the pitcher from her friend, she scolded her as well. "You should've made that bonehead help. He's just freaking standing there...doing *nothing*!"

Hannah smiled while she set the tray on the table, took the pitcher, and poured two glasses of tea before motioning for Melanie to sit down. "Sit and eat, hothead. Yelling at the guard is only raising your blood pressure. He could seriously care less."

Both ladies chuckled as Melanie took the covers off her food and began eating. Once again Hannah's sisters had made some of her favorite foods – chicken salad with apples and walnuts on romaine, whole grain rolls, cucumber salad, and a slice of homemade apple crisp. She took a deep breath, inhaling all the yummy goodness and smiled before digging in.

She was just about to take her first bite when Hannah uttered, "*Tost.*" Shrugging, Melanie took the bite off the fork floating before her mouth and waited for her friend to explain.

Looking side to side, Hannah leaned forward and quietly said, "I put a Silence Spell on your room. It should go undetected, but just in case, we're gonna make it quick and I'll remove it so no one questions what we're doing."

Melanie chuckled at Hannah's thorough explanation, knowing it was her nerves talking. The young witch had grown up making the best of a horrible situation. She had survived all the black magic and killings without turning dark. Melanie knew it was because Hannah had the strength of her mother and sisters. Joanie had always told Melanie if anything happened, she could count on Sarah Beth and all these years later it was still true.

Many times before her mother had died, when they'd been planning their escape, Melanie had asked if Hannah and her family were coming with them. Her mother's response was always the same. "They can't, honey. This is all they know, but they are good and with any luck will reform the *Dorcha*. We just need to pray for them, Meli Rose. Pray that they can overtake Cleland." Melanie was sad that her mother's prayers had not been answered but happy to see her childhood friend was still one of the good ones.

Melanie nodded her understanding but continued to eat as Hannah quickly explained. "Mom and few of the others are working on a plan. It seems like Cleland may suspect them, so it is taking longer than they anticipated, but she said to tell you she will do *everything* in her power to keep you safe."

Melanie saw the unshed tears in Hannah's eyes. Laying her fork on her plate, she placed both her hands over her friend's and smiled. "Tell her to keep herself and her family safe before worrying about me. Let's face it, if Cleland wants to go through with this, there's little any of us can do without outside help to stop him. I won't have any of you getting hurt on my account."

"Cut the shit, Meli. You know as well as I do Mom thinks of you as one of her own and thought of your mom like a sister. There's not a chance she's gonna go back on the promise she made to Joanie." Hannah gave a weak chuckle that was more sad than funny.

"Well, you need to make her see that she *has* to. I'll get out of this shithole one way or another and I *have* to know that y'all are okay when I do. If you need to, tell Sarah Beth to come see me."

"Oh, she'll be here with your dinner." Hannah's eyes were wide and almost smiling. "You better get ready, I'm sure she's gonna have a few choice words about your appraisal of the situation."

Both ladies laughed until they were tearing up. When they recovered, Hannah removed the spell and Melanie finished her lunch. Too soon, the guard opened the door and instructed Hannah it was time to go. They both stood and hugged before Hannah gathered up the dishes and headed towards the door. She winked over her shoulder as she disappeared into the hall and the door was once again shut and locked.

With nothing better to do, Melanie took a long hot shower, painted her toes with the horrible Pepto Bismol pink nail polish she found in the vanity, and settled down to read Wuthering Heights for the fourth or fifth time. She alternated between reading and dozing until a knock at the door alerted her to an incoming visitor. Sure it was Sarah Beth, she sat up cross-legged in the middle of the bed and waited.

Unfortunately, her anticipation at talking to the woman she considered her second mom turned to shock and then quickly anger when it was Cleland who entered her room. She watched the smile dissolve from his face and could only imagine it was a reaction to her own. Melanie did nothing to hide her disgust. She was, after all, the prisoner and he was her jailer. There was no way she would be nice and polite.

Nope. Not gonna happen.

Leaning on the same ancient cane topped with a skull carved from bone that Melanie remembered from her childhood, looking at her through the same watery blue eyes that had watched her while cutting out her mother's heart was the man she'd once called Grandpa. The man she now wanted to watch gasping for his last breath like a whale on the shore.

If his expression was any indication, Cleland had figured out what she was thinking without the benefit of reading her mind. Melanie had always been one of the few he couldn't read, along with her mother, Sarah Beth, Hannah, and all Hannah's sisters. There had been stories of others, but those witches had mysteriously disappeared. The only thing that kept Hannah and her family safe was their unique familial magic. Alone, each was an above average witch, but together they were a force with which to be reckoned.

Melanie knew the *Draoi* had kept them close, siphoning off bits of power to keep him going until he could find her. If he kept his theft to a minimum they would never know, their magic, after all, regenerated.

She also knew he would never do anything to harm them if he could help it. Since she hadn't had a child, the bloodline died with her, which meant Cleland's ability to steal power died as well. Sure, he could kill other witches and wizards and take their power, but it would be short lived and cause his followers to rebel. Yeah, her *seanathair* was no dummy. He knew he'd need Hannah and her family to keep him in power. All Melanie had to do was make sure he never found out they'd helped her all those years ago and were planning to help her now. Something told her old Cleland would give up a few of his magical infusers to make a point and that was *not* something she could live with.

Cleland finally spoke, ending the Mexican standoff between them. "You look well, dear."

Rolling her eyes, Melanie shook her head and waited.

Instead of speaking again, the *Draoi* made a huge production out of getting a chair, positioning it beside her bed, and sitting like the king he thought he was. After placing his cane across the end of her bed and unbuttoning his drab grey suit jacket, he again spoke, his tone still that of the grandfather she'd thought he was when she was a child. "I hope the coven is taking good care of you. I see the clothes I ordered fit. Is there anything else I can get for you?"

Snorting a sarcastic almost laugh, Melanie said, "Yeah, how about a get out of jail free card and the keys to a car?"

"Jail? Is that what you think this is, Meli Rose? Your prison? You could not be farther from the truth. You will have free reign over all the grounds, just as soon as I am sure you are ready. I want you to reacquaint yourself with the members and meet the new ones. This always has been and always will be your home. We are all just thrilled to have you back."

Melanie looked at Cleland like he had three heads and four horns while trying to figure out what game he was playing. She knew damn good and well he'd brought her to the coven to regain his power and the only way he could do that was to kill her. Maybe he was delusional enough to think she'd forgotten, so she decided to remind him that she was nobody's fool.

"Let's cut the shit, Cleland. I know why you brought me here and it wasn't for a good ole family reunion. At least we can be honest with each other after all these years. You're old. You need to replenish your power. You've tried siphoning and have probably even killed a few wizards along the way to keep your throne, but none of that's working anymore. It's not the same as killing a family member and bathing in their blood, right? And after all, when you kill your followers, you're thinning the herd and people might find the bodies. Am I right?"

"Oh my, dear, you have totally misjudged me. This reunion is not at all what you…" His words were cut off by the obnoxious trill of a cellphone ringing in his jacket pocket.

Holding up his index finger in the universal 'one minute' sign, Cleland proceeded to pull out the phone and answer the call. Melanie looked out the window, ignoring his side of the conversation until he said, "I'll be right there."

Jumping off the bed, she stood less than a foot in front of the man that had lived in her nightmares for almost twenty years and growled. "Oh, hell no. You're staying here until you tell me exactly what's going on."

He grinned and her palm itched with the need to smack the condescending look from his face. Then he snapped his fingers and his cane flew to his outstretched hand. Completely dismissing Melanie and ignoring her demand, the *Draoi* pushed back the chair he'd been sitting in, turned on his heel, and walked towards the door.

Never one to be snubbed, Melanie yelled, "I swear to the Goddess if you leave this room without answering my questions, I will take my own life. That would really screw up your sacrifice wouldn't it...*Grandpa*?" The last word was spoken with so much derision she reveled in the fact that he flinched.

Cleland took the last few steps to the door and knocked before turning to face her. For just a split second she saw the man that had bounced her on his knee and told her bedtime stories, but in the blink of an eye reality came crashing down around her and all she could see was the monster that murdered her mother. He spoke and for the first time she heard the low rumble of his age. "I have no intention of sacrificing you, Meli Rose. I have been presented with a far better proposition that will keep me in power and you breathing for hundreds of years. As far as harming yourself, do you really think I would take that chance?" He shook his head like she was a brick short of a load before continuing. "You, as well as your room, have been warded. You cannot even suffer a hang nail without immediately healing."

61

The door opened, Cleland stepped over the threshold and was gone before her brain could process what she'd heard. Running to catch the door before it closed, she tripped over the rug and caught the knob just as the lock clicked into place. She pounded on the door until her hands were bright red and burning while screaming until she lost her voice but no one came.

Tired, angry, and confused, Melanie threw herself across the bed and stared at the ceiling, trying to figure out what the senile old asshole had been talking about. The rest of the day was pretty much a bust. She had no idea what her grandfather was planning and for the most part was sick of thinking about it.

Melanie sat by the window at the back of her room, watching the younger children of the coven playing in the clearing. It reminded her of all the times she'd done the same thing, one of the only happy memories she still had from her time with the *Dorcha.* The smell of food brought her out her revelry. Turning, she expected to find Hannah but instead saw a tall, gangly teenager she didn't know with her food tray in his hands. Immediately worried about her friends and unsure whether she could trust the young man enough to ask questions, she simply smiled and made her way to the table. Thankfully, he was chatty. In less than a minute, Melanie found out his name was Joshua, he was almost eighteen, Hannah and her family were attending the weekly ritual and would resume bringing her food in the morning. She smiled at his naivety and hoped he would always be as carefree as he was in that moment.

The next few days flew by. She saw Hannah a few times but never alone and always just long enough to drop off her food or clean clothes. She could see in her friend's eyes that she wanted to talk, but her every move was being monitored. It seemed that Cleland wasn't taking any chances.

By the morning of the Blood Moon, Melanie had decided it was time to take drastic measures. From the moment she'd awoken with a bag over her head, she'd held out hope that her magic could remain suppressed, but time was running out. There was no way she could continue to sit idly by and wait for the inevitable. It was time to bring her magic back. She'd tried to come up with another solution, knowing full well that it was playing right into the *Draoi's* hands, but it was the only chance she had to save herself without anyone she cared about getting hurt in the process.

The one and only time Cleland had visited her, he'd mentioned a ward had been placed on her and her room that would keep her from harm. That was going to make unmasking her magic more difficult but not impossible. Rising from her seat at the window, Melanie collected the knife she'd stolen from last night's dinner out from under her mattress and made her way to the bathroom. Carefully, she shut and locked the door, then started the shower.

Disrobing to just her bra and panties, she located the Charm of Cerridwen that had been tattooed on her left hip the day of her eighteenth birthday. The tattoo, done by a very powerful shaman, had replaced the physical charm Sarah Beth had given her the day she'd run from the coven. It had been the only way Melanie knew she would always have protection from the *Draoi*.

And we all know how that worked out.

She cleaned both the knife and her hip with rubbing alcohol. The shaman had explained that if she ever wanted to use her magic again, all she needed to do was recite the spell while severing the Celtic Circle from the Tree of Life it surrounded in two places. He'd further explained it had to be a permanent separation so she would need to remove two small pieces of inked skin.

In any other situation that would've been no big deal. Sure, it would hurt, but Melanie had a pretty high tolerance for pain and knew it would heal. It was the fact that she would have to move faster than the spell Cleland had placed on her person that had her pulse beating faster than usual.

Summoning her courage, she took a deep breath, laid the knife against the edge of the tattoo and exhaled as she counted to five. Striking with incredible accuracy and a speed she knew was powered by her nerves, Melanie used the sharp tip of the knife to remove two miniscule sections of her inked skin from where the base of the tree connected with the circle. She whispered, *bhaint agus a chur ar ais.*

The tiny incisions burned like hell and began to heal before she could grab the peroxide to clean the wound. She watched as the skin knit back together but this time without the ink. Magic filled her being. Tiny black dots danced before her eyes and she felt lightheaded as the magical part of her being took its first breath of fresh air in almost eighteen years. It should have been a happy time, but all Melanie could think about was what Cleland planned to do with her power. More than a little sadness filled her heart as she thought about the way he would turn her beautiful white magic into something ugly and unrecognizable if he were ever to get his slimy fingers on it.

Within five minutes her cuts were healed and the pain was gone. All that was left to do was to place a Camouflage Spell on the tattoo and her magic. It wouldn't keep Cleland from taking her power, but it would make it a damn sight harder and that might be the few seconds she needed to get away.

Shutting off the shower steaming up the room, she redressed, and returned to her bedroom. She immediately knew someone had been in the room. The air felt different...disturbed. It was one of the many sensations she would have to get used to now that her magic was functional again. Looking for signs of the intruder, she found a large black box with a huge red ribbon and bow sitting on her bed. Using her rusty powers, Melanie inspected the package and found it held no enchantments and had been placed on her bed by one of the guards.

Carefully removing the bow and unwinding the ribbon, she laid the lid of the box to the side and unwrapped the tissue paper. She gasped when she saw the crystal covered ivory silk bodice. It was truly a work of art. As she lifted the gown from the box, it only became lovelier. The skirt was long and flowing with groups of the same beautiful crystals artfully placed to form dianthus blossoms, the flower that had been blooming the day she was born...or so she'd been told.

Holding the strapless gown against her body, she spun around in circles, enjoying the movement of the fabric and the way the light danced off the crystals. On one of her revolutions, she caught sight of herself in the full length mirror by her wardrobe. She smiled at the reflection, wishing to the Heavens that Jace could see her in something so elegant, then wondered if she would ever see him again. Shaking away her maudlin thoughts, she turned towards the bed to return the gown to the box. Melanie had no idea why anyone would send her such a gorgeous dress just to bleed all over and figured it was another of Cleland's head games.

She'd just replaced the lid on the box when there was a knock at her door. With her returned powers, she knew it was the *Draoi,* and he was accompanied by another wizard with far less power but just as much bad attitude. The door swung open and in came Cleland, closely followed by a tall, olive-skinned man with inky black hair and a dead expression. In any other situation, Melanie imagined he would be good looking but the stench of black magic and servitude to an evil leader coated his aura with dark black fog. She was just about to dismiss him and begin interrogating her grandfather when she finally recognized him. It was Damon, a boy from her past, now grown into a man and serving the one person in the world they'd all sworn to kill.

Giving him a look of pure disgust, she was shocked when he smiled and winked. Rolling her eyes, she ignored him and turned her attention to Cleland. "To what do I owe the honor? I thought you'd forgotten about me. I seem to remember you promising to come back and explain what your plans for me were, but that was three days ago. Whatcha been up to?" Melanie purposely spoke as informally as possible, knowing full well it would infuriate the *Draoi*. He took his position very seriously and wanted to be treated with the utmost 'respect' at all times, especially from his granddaughter and in the presence of his second.

Yeah, well, he can spit in one hand and wish in the other to see which fills up first.

The lift of his eyebrows and the way the corners of his mouth turned downward let Melanie know she'd hit the mark and her little heart sang. She smiled the sweetest smile she could and took a seat on the edge of her bed, preparing for whatever bullshit Cleland was about to spread around. The *Draoi* quickly recovered and just as she'd predicted, began to speak with the voice and charisma of a televangelist.

"You look well, Meli Rose. I apologize for leaving you alone, but I had many things to prepare and oversee for this evening's festivities." Looking over her shoulder, he continued. "I see you received my gift. If it needs any adjustments, please have the guards call for my seamstress. She will be happy to assist you."

He moved to the table and took a seat. It was the first time in her life she could remember him looking tired. Hopefully he would stay that way. Deciding it was time to get some answers, Melanie moved past Damon, who had yet to speak, and sat down across from Cleland.

"So, what exactly have you got cooked up for tonight, *Cleland*?" She used his given name, adding a little punch to her voice and was tickled pink as the snide grin slid from his face.

Pushing her advantage, she asked, "What's with the gown? I thought all the sacrifices had to wear a white robe of tradition."

In the blink of an eye, the smirk was back and a fire shone in Cleland's dead eyes. He shook his head and tsk'd before responding. "Oh, Meli Rose, you always were one for the dramatic. Although, I will admit to putting the Great Sacrifice on the list of possible solutions to draining the power of our coven, but it was most definitely at the bottom. What I have planned for you will keep both of us alive for years."

"Cut the crap! Whatever the scheme, the answer is no. Now, you said I could have free reign and so far I'm still locked in this damn room. What gives?"

Chuckling with an air of authority that made the little hairs at the back of her neck stand on end, the *Draoi* stood and walked towards the door. "Oh, Meli Rose, I do so enjoy our talks but let me make one thing clear, it is not up to you to accept or decline. You will do as I say. And as far as free reign goes, after tonight's ceremony you will have it, of that you can be sure. Now, try on your gown, make sure it's perfect, Hannah will be along in just a few minutes to help you with your hair and makeup."

Obviously done with her, the *Draoi* nodded his head and Damon fell in behind him like the good minion he appeared to be. Hell, Melanie had even forgotten the guy was there, he'd been so quiet. Not willing to let Cleland get away without answers, she growled, "Do not leave this room without telling me what in the sam hell is going on."

Already in the hall with the door shutting the *Draoi* called out, "Oh darling, I'm sorry I forgot to tell you…it's your wedding day. You and Damon will be married at the height of the Blood Moon."

Son of a bitch! I didn't see that one coming.

CHAPTER FIVE

"Who knew there were so many Blackthorn trees?"

A smack to the back of Jace's head was quickly followed by a growl. "Would've been easier had you remembered the red blossoms before this morning, *dumbass*."

"Yeah, sorry 'bout that." He hung his head and hoped he hadn't thrown away his only chance at finding his mate.

"Y'all give the guy a break. He's worried about Melanie, frustrated at being away from her, and it's not like every one of you hasn't screwed up just as bad, if not worse, in your lives." Kyra scolded.

"But *mo chroi'*," Royce began but was quickly cut off.

"But nothing, Roy, I mean it." The look the tiny witch gave her much bigger mate was scary and the way the giant of a Guardsman buckled under her glare was comical.

Jace almost bust a gut when Lance quipped, "Be careful, grandpa. I'm still waiting for her to turn you into a toad."

"Dammit, Lance," Royce bellowed but was cut off as laughter filled the cave where they were camping.

"Seriously, big brother, when are you gonna learn?" Rory chuckled.

Giving up, Royce grunted something unintelligible under his breath and stepped out of the cave. The laughter died down as the Guardsmen packed up their belongings. Kyra sat in the back, working on a spell to scry for not only Melanie but the use of *Dorcha* magic. Jace looked at all the men he was proud to call brethren. Some of them he'd known since his first transformation, others he'd met in just the last week but none of that mattered, they were all there to help him find his mate. They were all family.

"Whatcha daydreaming about, loverboy?" Liam asked and he bumped Jace with his shoulder on the way by.

"Nothing…Everything…Oh hell…Melanie."

Liam chuckled as he threw his pack on the pile with the others. "Yeah, well, tell me something new. That shit's been going on for months."

"I know. It's just that…"

"It's just that you're afraid we're not gonna make it in time, that *you're* not going to make it in time." Rory cut in from somewhere behind him.

Before the young Guardsman could get turned around, the Leader of the Blue Thunder Force was standing next to him with his hand on his shoulder. "Look, Jace, I don't have a mate yet, but I've seen firsthand what some of these guys have gone through to claim theirs…"

There were murmurs and grunts of agreement from all the mated Guardsmen and "Hell, yeah" from the little witch before Rory continued. "You'll find her. Have faith. My one piece of advice is, and remember this is coming from an unmated dragon, make it official as soon as you can. Don't let her get away from you again. You got a keeper there. I never believed the crap they told us when we were young about the Universe not making mistakes and Fate not being denied but looking at Dev, Roy, and Lance, I gotta say if those losers get to spend eternity with great women, then you and I've got it made."

Rory ducked just in time to avoid being hit by the flying boot Lance had thrown and a half eaten apple courtesy of Devon, but the punch delivered courtesy of his big brother landed right in the middle of his chest. Jace watched while Rory tried not to flinch but finally gave in with a half-laugh, half-wheeze. Once again the cave was filled with laughter, thankfully lightening the young Guardsman's mood.

"Paybacks are a bitch, big bro." Rory wheezed.

"Aren't they though, little brother." Royce snickered, looking incredibly pleased with himself.

"As fun as all this is, we need to get moving. We've wasted enough time chasing our tails. I'm ready to find Jace's mate and kick some dark wizard ass. What about y'all?" Kellan's proclamation shocked the group into silence. For him to speak more than three words at one time was a miracle.

Nodding, Rory made the call. "You heard the man, let's get outta here."

Kellen led the way and by mid-morning they had reached an entire hillside and valley covered in red blossomed Blackthorn trees. Jace's best guess was about thirty-square miles were covered with the black barked trees covered in blood red flowers.

Kyra dropped to the ground, pulled out all her witchy goodies, and began what she'd earlier explained was scrying. Kellan was once again meditating or focusing or whatever it was called, looking for any sign of Melanie and the men that had kidnapped her. For the next two hours, Jace paced, then looked over Kyra's shoulder, then paced some more. He would've gone to look over Kellan's shoulder, too, but had to admit the guy still scared the crap out of him. The young Guardsman would spend most of his life indebted to the scarred man for all he'd done to find his mate, of that there was no doubt. But there was something deep in his eyes that was just scary as hell, it made Jace jumpy.

"Deep breaths, bro, deep breaths. You're gonna stroke out and then we're gonna have a big ass bronze dragon trampling the countryside." Liam teased.

"I know but the more time that passes, the harder it gets."

"Look, I have no clue what you're going through, but you better buck up buttercup. We're gonna find her and you better be ready to say all the right things and make all the right choices. 'Cause something tells me your mate will take no indecision, especially after the last few days."

"You're right." Jace took a deep breath and held it for a minute while he concentrated on their silent mating bond. Slowly exhaling, he pulled from the strength of his dragon who gladly pushed as well. Together they looked for any sign that Melanie was okay. For the first time, other than her cryptic message, he could *feel* her. It wasn't as strong as it had been in the past and definitely felt like it would break at any moment, but it was the spark he needed to get his shit together.

Opening his eyes, he started to yell his joy to his brethren, but Kyra beat him to the punch. "Hot damn, I got a line on a shitload of black magic. It's got to be them!" The little witch was all but jumping up and down as she packed up her supplies and yelled for her mate.

Kellan's shout came on the heels of Kyra's. "I got her. She's about twenty miles due north of here, underground, and pissed as shit from what I'm picking up." He paused and looked right at Jace, furrowing his brow, and frowning for just a second. "Something's changed. I can sense her magic now and it's *strong.* Strong like Kyra strong and just as white and pure. No wonder the *Draoi* wanted your girl. She's got chops."

Jace knew he should be worried at Kellan's proclamation but instead he was proud, prouder than he'd ever been. He'd known she was strong but had been worried how a human would fit in with a clan of dragon shifters and their families. He'd seen how Kyndel, Grace, and Dr. Malone, mates of his Commander and other Guardsmen, had dealt with it. But those ladies, although human, still had 'special' qualities that allowed them to deal with mates that could turn into dragons. The knowledge that Melanie was also magical was the best news he'd gotten in a long time.

Unable to wait a moment longer, he looked to Rory and Royce who were conferring with the other Guardsmen and yelled, "Can we get the hell outta dodge? I gotta girl to save."

They all laughed and shook their heads as Rory answered. "Give us a minute, kid. I keep telling you we're gonna get your girl back, don't blow the game in the last few minutes."

Jace smirked at Rory's sports analogy as he made his way over to the powwow. It was quickly decided that they would follow the directions Kyra and Kellan agreed upon. Once they were within two miles of their destination, the entire group would find a place to hang out until the sun was completely down. Once it was truly dark, Pearce and Declan would call forth their dragons and take to the sky. The deep midnight blue color of their beasts would provide the perfect cover for them to scout the area with the highest concentration of dark magic that Kyra had located.

"I'll go limb to limb through the trees. I somehow doubt those dimwitted dark wizards will expect a black panther to be part of the gang." Jace chuckled at Max's incredible arrogance. On anyone else it would be irritating but on the King of the Big Cats, it seemed fitting.

Trekking through the forest of Blackthorn trees seemed to take forever. Rory and Royce had agreed that they should not use their enhanced speed to avoid the *Dorcha* sensing the use of dragon magic. The closer they got to their target, the stronger the stench of black magic became. It wasn't overpowering, like when they'd been chasing Andrew. This time it was a sprinkling that slowly became a mist that he knew would become a dense fog before it was over.

The trees were so dense and the red blossoms so plentiful in the part of the forest they were in that the shards of sunlight, which had been breaking through during the day, simply ceased to exist. That coupled with the growing prevalence of dark magic caused an eerie sensation to skitter down Jace's spine and his dragon chuffed a warning.

Cue the creepy music, I swear I'm in a Wes Craven movie.

He was just about to share the joke with Liam when Kellan's fist flew into the air, the military signal for halt. The Guardsmen paused and waited. Their tension spiked in the few seconds it took for the retired marine to turn around and address the group.

"The clearing we've been looking for is just over that ridge." Kellan motioned over his shoulder with his thumb. *"We need to wait here. The sun will be down in approximately two and a half hours. It will be dark enough for dragons in about four."*

"All right, you heard the man, grab a bite to eat and get some rest. Only four hours until we kick Dorcha *ass and bring Melanie home."* Rory looked right at Jace when he mentioned the young Guardsman's mate and the rest of the Guardsmen nodded their agreement before breaking formation and dropping their packs.

During the next few hours, Jace ate, paced, questioned Kyra to see if she'd come up with anything new, and basically drove everyone crazy. The sun went down and Rory called them all together. After rehashing their plan to infiltrate the coven. Jace had to keep reminding himself to pay attention. All he could think about was getting to Melanie and killing anyone and anything that stood in his path. His dragon roared in agreement.

"I just want to make sure y'all understand that the clearing is some sort of 'holy' place for the *Dorcha*. Black magic is permeating damn near every rock, tree, and molecule of that place. Blood has been spilt there, *lots* of blood. It's a place of power for them. Here are protection amulets for each of you." The little witch began handing all thirteen members of their search party the small silver discs with leather cords she'd spelled while they'd been waiting. "Just be careful."

Royce put his arm around Kyra's shoulders, pulling her close to his side, and dropped a kiss on the top of her head. The scene made Jace envious for the time when he would again hold Melanie in his arms and proclaim his love for her. He also wanted to kick his own ass for all the time he'd wasted tiptoeing around instead of claiming her as his own and keeping her safe.

I will be correcting that situation just as soon as possible.

The feel of magic on his skin drew his attention. Jace turned just in time to see two full grown dark blue dragons take flight. His own dragon growled and blew smoke, pushing to be allowed to do the same thing. Only the reassurance of the man that the beast would be allowed to avenge their mate's abduction kept the winged warrior at bay.

Rory had given the signal for them to get into formation. Max went from man to panther in the blink of an eye. With the flick of his tail and a flash of glowing green eyes, the Leo disappeared into the forest. Werecats and dragons could not share in mindspeak as humans, but recently it had been discovered they could while in animal form. It was decided Max would relay anything he saw to Declan and Pearce and they would inform Rory.

Kellan had just started to lead their group through the forest when Declan and Pearce located the clearing. They reported seeing a large circle drawn with salt and ash surrounding a stone altar with thousands of black candles illuminating the entire area. As they continued to fly over, witches and wizards dressed in gowns and suits exited a large stone doorway.

"We need to move our asses!" Jace bellowed.

"Calm down, young'un, can't go rushing in there and risk getting your mate hurt. Take a deep breath. Max is almost in position." Rory commanded.

Jace growled his irritation but stayed in formation. He listened intently as Declan and Pearce relayed everything they saw. For the hundredth time in the last hour Jace focused all his strength and all the power of his dragon on their silent mating bond. He prayed to the Heavens for help. He begged the Ancients for guidance. He pleaded with Fate and Destiny to show him the way to his mate. He did everything in his considerable power to make contact with the woman that had become the center of his world.

Declan's report broke through his prayers. *"Max is hanging on a limb just above the coven. He reports a classically dressed old man leaning heavily on a cane and a young man in a tux have just exited the tunnel. He's sure from the way the rest of the attendees are bowing and scraping that the older gentleman is the* Draoi. *And best guess is the other is his second."* The Guardsmen in dragon form paused and Jace doubled his efforts to reach Melanie.

It was Pearce's voice that sounded in Jace's mind after just a few moments of silence. *"A wizard, I'm guessing is their Holy Man, just entered the circle and is chanting. Everyone but the* Draoi *are watching the priest. The old man is focused on the mouth of the tunnel, like he's waiting for the guest of honor."*

After a brief pause, he added, *"The guest of honor has arrived and she is gorgeous. I guess it's her wedding day from the look of the dazzling gown...Son of a bitch! It's Melanie!"*

Jace didn't have a chance to respond because as he opened his mouth, Melanie's voice sounded in his mind. It was stronger than before but still distant and her words made him run through the forest, roaring her name.

"Jace, I sure as hell hope you can hear me. I really need your help. I have to figure a way out of here or you need to show up with the cavalry. Within thirty minutes, I'm gonna be married to a douchebag named Damon. Please don't let me become Mrs. Douchebag."

CHAPTER SIX

She knew she sounded like a damsel in distress begging to be saved by her knight in shining armor and that went against everything she believed in, but with no other prospects to be found, she was willing to swallow her pride. If she were forced to marry Damon, then she would truly be trapped for the rest of her life, which for a witch can be a *very* long time. There was no such thing as divorce in the coven. When they say until death do you part…they were being literal. Melanie was also sure that Cleland would have rigged the ceremony with some mystical trapdoor. Something promising dire consequences to not only her but anyone she cared about if she tried to run.

Looking in the mirror, admiring her stunning gown, trying to forget who purchased it for her and what it stood for, she admired the beautiful way Hannah's sister, Alicia, had styled her short dark hair and applied her makeup. Melanie wished she was wearing it for a different man at a different ceremony far away from her crazy ass grandfather and his mindless followers.

Shaking her head, Melanie turned away from the mirror and stared out the window into the dark night, trying with all her might to teleport somewhere, anywhere but where she was at that moment. Of course, nothing happened thanks to the Dampening Spell she'd felt the *Draoi* put on the room night before last. She knew they would be coming to get her at any moment and cursed that she hadn't been able to escape. Every plan she, Hannah, and Sarah Beth had come up with either required more time to pull off or would expose the people she held most dear as traitors to the *Dorcha*. There was no way she could let that happen.

Jace was all she'd been able to think about for the last few hours, not that thinking of him was a new occurrence, since the moment she'd first seen him, he'd been a constant distraction. It was as if he'd invaded her brain in the same way he'd captured her heart all those months ago. She'd been mentally kicking herself for never telling the amazing man what she felt for him. It wasn't that there hadn't been time or that she feared rejection. There was something deep in her soul that said he held the same feelings for her. No matter how she looked at it, she couldn't come up with a good reason why she hadn't told him, just that she hadn't and now she feared it was too late.

Panic made it hard for Melanie to breathe as the knock at the door she'd been dreading sounded. Without waiting for her to answer, the young man that had delivered her dinner on several occasions opened the door and walked into her room. He was a good kid, misguided, and sure to die a horrible death led by Cleland, but a good kid all the same. She hated that she couldn't remember his name.

"Are you ready to go, Miss Whelan?" He smiled brightly, like she should be happy about being forced to marry Damon. Then she realized neither he nor anyone in the *Dorcha*- aside from said groom, the *Draoi*, and Hannah and her family- knew that this was anything but another in a long line of arranged marriages in the coven's history.

"As ready as I'll ever be, kid." She mumbled under her breath and walked towards the door.

Ever the gentleman, her escort stood waiting in the doorway, his arm crooked for her to hold onto. As they walked down the cavernous stone hallway, they passed members of the *Draoi's* guard every twenty feet or so.

Apparently, Grandpa doesn't trust me as much as he professes to.

Candlelight shone from the wide opening at the end of the passage. As they drew closer, Melanie recognized the scent of steaming herbs and the sound of chanting. The words were familiar and just as she'd guessed, was a spell binding her to the coven as soon as she and Damon had consummated their union. A chuckle that sounded more like the maniacal laughter of a comic book villain bubbled past her lips as they reached the edge of the threshold leading to the *Dorcha's* sacred circle.

Well, here goes nothing.

The toe of her satin slipper had just touched down on the inside of the salt and ash circle when a roar shook the trees all around them. A collective gasp rose from the coven as they all searched for the origin of the disruption. It seemed to go on and on, echoing off the hills and mountains surrounding the valley and the hallowed ground.

A knowing look crossed Cleland's face, then quickly was followed by fear and loathing as he whispered something to Damon. The younger man nodded, turned, and strode in her direction, a look of determination darkening his face. Again the trees trembled and quaked as another roar tore through the air. This time much closer and infinitely louder, causing blood red blossoms to cover the Sacred Circle and her ears to ring.

Damon appeared in front of her as she surveyed the inky blackness surrounding their gathering. Without preamble, he hoisted her into the air and unceremoniously threw her over his shoulder. Stunned for a just a second, Melanie began to kick and scream, demanding to be released.

Obviously unmoved by the abuse she was bestowing upon his chest and back, Damon quickly moved towards the back side of the circle and the darkness of the forest. Lifting her head, Melanie looked for anything she could use as a weapon. Throwing out her hand, she grabbed the base of one of the candelabras standing throughout the clearing. It was heavier than she realized and instead of ending up in her hand, it hit the ground, sparking a fire. Fear for all the people in attendance made her scream even louder to be released. She panicked as she watched it spread towards the witches and wizards that were frantically trying to reenter the coven.

Another roar split the air at the same time that nine huge figures burst into the clearing. There, standing almost a hundred feet away, looking like a Roman General leading his troops stood the man of her dreams. He gripped a long broadsword, poised and ready to take on all oncomers.

His blue eyes glowed with rage as he searched the crowd. Their eyes met and she felt more emotions than she'd ever imagined, then heard the voice she'd feared she might never hear again. *"Hold on, mo chroi'. Hold on."*

Her heart skipped a beat and the breath fled her lungs as Jace threw back his head and roared to the Heavens. Her shock was palpable. She tried to reason away what she'd just witnessed as a hallucination from the stress of the previous days and was almost successful until Jace moved so quickly, dodging the spells being thrown that her eyes couldn't track the movement. It was then she realized all the men that came with him were also moving as if by magic.

What the hell?

Damon broke through the salt and ash circle, running as fast as he could with her slung over his shoulder. Jace continued his pursuit, but the dark wizard threw spell after spell over his shoulder, causing her man to lose ground every time he had to swerve out of the way.

Unable to slow Damon down, Melanie tried to think of something to help Jace when the wizard made a sharp left then a right and dropped through a hole in the ground. She screamed as they fell through the air and grunted when his shoulder dug into her midsection as they hit the ground. In no time at all, the wizard was once again running, this time through a dark, dirty tunnel lit only by the occasional torch hanging from the wall.

Footsteps pounded behind them but sounded softer than she imagined her six-foot-three-inch savior would make. As the thought crossed her mind, a set of glowing green eyes came into view. Two seconds later the huge Black Panther those eyes belonged to came into view. Melanie gasped, the cat snarled and for the first time since the craziness began, Damon stumbled.

Afraid she was going to end up face first in the dirt, Melanie squeezed her eyes closed and threw out her hands to break the fall she was sure was to come. When nothing happened, she opened her eyes just in time to see that the panther had caught up to them. She could've sworn the big cat smiled as he swiped and hissed at her captor. It seemed the panther was pushing Damon in the direction he wanted the wizard to go instead of trying to hurt him.

Okay, I've had enough for today.

Unable to maintain the awkward posture she'd been forced into and sure she was losing her mind, Melanie fell forward and hung on for the ride, listening to the snarling of the beautiful panther dogging Damon's every step. A cool breeze hit her bare legs where her gown had ridden up while she'd been riding on Damon's shoulder. Needing to see where they had ended up, she once again lifted her head, this time propping her hands just above the evil wizard's bum.

The panther was still in pursuit but falling back. Damon maneuvered the trees until he reached another, smaller clearing Melanie remembered from her childhood. Light from the Blood Moon showed little had changed in all those years. The wizard stopped, placed Melanie on the large stump in the middle of the glade, and began pacing a groove in the forest floor.

Leaves rustled overhead right before a group of the *Draoi's* guard stepped into the moonlight. She recognized Putz One and Two from her original kidnapping but none of the others were familiar. Damon immediately went to them, speaking the language of their ancestors. Melanie wished she remembered more of the old dialect, as it was, she could only pick out certain words.

Unbeknownst to the wizards, a branch over their heads creaked. Melanie's eyes flew towards the noise and found the panther precariously perched above them with a look that reminded her of the Cheshire cat from Alice in

84

Wonderland. Smiling at the cat and chuckling at the thought of him pouncing on the heads of the men that had held her hostage, Melanie almost fell off the stump when Jace led the same nine men towards the *Dorcha*.

The wizards turned as one unit and began firing spells at Jace and his friends. The men who looked like the NFL on steroids easily avoided the magical bolts and continued their march to end the wizards. Melanie looked up in time to see the panther land on two of the evil magicians. Sliding off the stump, she took cover to avoid being hit by ricochet magic but watched the action while trying to keep tabs on Jace.

It looked as though Jace and his friends were going to defeat the wizards and Melanie wanted to stand up and cheer. But true to her recent luck, as members of the *Dorcha* fell, a whole new set of the *Draoi's* guard appeared. One wizard, Samuel that Melanie remembered from her youth, a *Dorcha* more evil than most, snuck behind Jace's back and took aim.

"Jace! Behind you!" Melanie screamed as loud as she could.

The world seemed to move in slow motion, Jace spun around, Samuel pulled back his arm and began to chant. The wizard's arm flew forward as Jace thrust his broadsword. Magic bounced off Jace's blade, lighting the clearing with sparks of black magic. The few that touched Melanie's bare arms and face stung like acid, and she wondered how the men continued to fight with the spent magic raining down on them…but fight they did.

Out of thin air, Samuel pulled a sword of his own, meeting Jace's strikes one for one. The battle waged on with Jace and his friends obviously the better of the two groups. She searched for a way to stop the endless supply of *Dorcha*, all ready to fall in battle.

Melanie tried to think of some way to help. Her magic burned in her veins, begging to help the man she now knew she loved, but it had been years since she'd cast spell. Hundreds of pieces of incantations sped through her mind, none of them complete. She feared it was only a matter of time before Jace and his friends could no longer fend off the hoards that continued to come at them.

A *thump* to the ground at her back had Melanie spinning around as the Black Panther who'd chased them through the tunnel hit the ground. The cat sprung over her head and entered the fight, taking out one wizard after another, but even with the giant feline's help, the *Dorcha* still outnumbered the good guys.

Magic cracked and lit the night sky as the wizards tried to end the battle once and for all. Melanie scanned the scene before her, looking for Jace and all of his friends. She had just breathed a sigh of relief that they were all still standing when a powerful magic tore through the clearing, sending streaks of electricity in every direction. The warriors and wizards stood completely still in the position they'd been in when the spell was cast.

She looked to Jace and saw rage burning in his eyes and could feel him fighting against the spell with all that he was. Looking for the source of the magic, Melanie caught a glimpse of a shadow speeding through the trees. Torn between following the wizard and staying with the man that had brought the cavalry to save her, she opted to stay and see what she could do to remove the spell that was holding them captive.

Before she could act, the air filled with a fresh clean magic that resembled her own but was also very different. It felt as if hundreds of butterflies were landing on her skin. Sure it was safe but not willing to let Jace or his friends face the new magic alone. Melanie used one of the few spells she remembered in its entirety.

Closing her eyes, she focused all her magic and whispered, *"A bheith inithe."*

The familiar feeling of her own magic surrounded her. She opened her eyes but immediately wanted to close them again. The removal spell she'd used had worked but unfortunately had removed the wizards and not Jace and his friends. Frantically trying to remember another incantation, the feel of butterflies once again touched her skin but this time was coupled with an energy that vibrated the ground beneath her feet.

She locked eyes with a still frozen Jace whose expression still harbored anger but had softened. His voice sounded in her head. *"This is not the way I wanted to tell you."*

"What are you talking..."

Melanie never finished her sentence. She found it hard to draw her next breath. As she looked on, the man that she'd already given her heart to transformed into a full grown bronze dragon.

Well, I'll be damned was her last thought as Melanie Whelan fainted for the first time in her life.

CHAPTER SEVEN

"What the holy hell is taking so long?" Jace growled.

"I swear we've spent this entire trip telling you to chill out and I'm saying it again…chill out. Pearce and Devon are taking care of her. It looks like she just fainted, which makes sense since she came face to face with a full grown dragon." Royce chuckled and Jace imagined punching his mentor in the face.

"You really should learn to shield better. I'll let your insolence go…this time, since your mate is still unconscious, but I promise retribution when we're all back home."

Jace knew he should feel bad for being disrespectful to Royce but was too worried about Melanie to care about what punishment the older Guardsman would concoct.

"And anyway because I transformed when I did, the spell was broken and y'all were able to gather up a few of the remaining Dorcha. *That should count for something, right?"*

"It does, Jace. You know the old man is just jerking your chain." Lance chuckled.

"Yeah, I know…"

"But you still feel responsible for Melanie's condition. That's the part you have to get over. Trust me, I know how hard it is. I want to wrap Sam and Syd in bubble wrap and lock them in the house so nothing ever happens to them, but let's be real…is that really gonna happen? Hell no! Sam would kick my ass and Syd would hold me down. Your mating bond is strong, right?"

"Yeah. So? What if she's pissed at me when she wakes?"

Lance barked out a laugh. *"Brother, you're gonna screw up on a daily basis. Sometimes she'll laugh it off and sometimes she'll be madder than a wet hen, so I'm gonna pass along a piece of advice that was given to me by the always wise Zen Master Walsh. Love her with everything you are. Love her like there will be no tomorrow. Love her like your life depends on it....because let me assure you...it does."*

"Yeah, I guess you're right."

Lance sighed and Jace could hear the beginnings of exasperation in his tone. *"You know there's nothing physically wrong with her and that Pearce's diagnosis of extreme exhaustion is spot on, right?"*

"Yeah, but..."

"There are no 'yeah but's' young'un. It is what it is. This is who we are and the Universe knows what She's doing when She makes our mates. They are beautiful, strong, and able to put up with our bullshit." The jokester of the bunch was laughing so hard at his own joke that he had to pause, which made Jace smile whether he wanted to or not.

"Amen!" Kyra added out loud. "At least ten times a day I think about smacking Roy upside the head with an iron skillet."

Every Guardsman within earshot started laughing, finally forcing Jace to join in.

"It looks like Melanie is waking up, loverboy." Pearce's comment had the younger Guardsman jumping out of his chair and running towards the bedroom.

Not even bothering to knock, Jace threw open the door and rushed to Melanie's side. Her color looked great and she seemed to be resting comfortably. No matter how many times he told himself not to touch her, to let her rest and just sit by her side, he couldn't stop his hand from holding hers, nor his thumb from rubbing circles on the back of her hand. It was just like every time they touched, electricity popped and crackled between them. He felt the current run through his body and fill his soul with the recognition of its other half.

When they were finally alone, Jace placed a kiss on her forehead, pushing his healing powers through their mating link, willing her to wake up. He was ready to bargain his soul and that of his dragon for just one more glimpse into her beautiful hazel eyes when she mumbled in her sleep.

Leaning forward, Jace placed his ear right above her pouty pink lips and waited intently for her to speak again. His patience paid off when after several seconds she murmured, "I love you, Jace. I'm just sorry I never got to tell you."

Remembering that Pearce had said there was no physical damage, Jace could no longer resist. He slid his arms under her body and carefully lifted her onto his lap. Cradling her like the precious gift she was, Jace took her scent deep into his lungs, smiling as his dragon rolled onto its back and purred with contentment. He rubbed the tip of his nose along the side of her neck, placing a gentle kiss behind her ear to mark her with his scent, just as she'd marked his heart the first time she'd smiled in his direction. Melanie stirred in her sleep, curling closer into his chest, her hands curling into fists that gripped his T-shirt, holding him as close as he held her.

Her unconscious recognizes me as her mate.

Jace was happier than dragon in flight and listened as she once again uttered her love for him. Placing his lips against the soft curvature of her ear he whispered, "I love you more than the stars in the sky, Melanie Rose Whelan. If you would just open your eyes, I'd make you mine for all time."

Jace sat for hours just holding his mate, loving the feel of her in his arms, and planning every detail of their very long lives together. In the wee hours of the morning, he carefully placed her back on the bed and laid down beside her, curling his body around hers to keep her close and safe. Sometime before the sun came up, the young Guardsman fell into a deep sleep. He dreamt of sweet little girls with dark brown curls and hazel eyes chasing rowdy little boys with blond hair and blue eyes, their squeal of delight filling the meadow.

A tickle at the corner of his lips caused his dreams to fade into the background. The tender touch grew more intense as it moved to his jawline then to his ear, leaving a path of desire in its wake. His eyes popped open when Melanie's breath bathed his ear and she whispered, "If you don't wake up soon, I'm gonna be forced to find someone else to take advantage of."

Grinning from ear to ear, Jace gripped her tight to his chest and answered, "You just try to get out of this bed."

Melanie lifted her head and looked him right in the eye. He could see the laughter shining back at him and how hard she was working to keep a straight face. He decided to play along and waited to see what she was up to. The wait was more than worth it.

"A dragon, huh?" Her shoulders bounced and he felt her tummy moving against his as she fought to control her laughter.

Never one to be outdone, Jace cocked an eyebrow and responded, "A witch, huh?"

Melanie's laugh was music to his ears, a sound a few days ago he believed he might never hear again. It was contagious and beautiful and so completely her.

"Yeah, about that," she said as soon as she'd recovered enough to speak.

He saw the change in her demeanor immediately. Melanie was afraid he would be upset with her for keeping secrets. Not wanting her to be anything but happy, Jace placed his index finger against her lips and shook his head.

"There's nothing to explain. We all have secrets, as you saw. I was going to tell you about a hundred times and every time I either chickened out or one of us was called away. Are you sure you're okay with what you saw?"

"Okay? Of course, I'm okay with it. It's who you are and explains *so* much."

He breathed a huge sigh of relief just as she added, "I figured *you'd* be pissed with *me*? But honestly…"

Once again he silenced her with a finger to her lips and laughed when she pretended to bite him. "There's nothing to explain. It's obvious you're nothing like your *seanathair.* And the witch thing is no big deal. Kyra, Royce's mate, is the daughter of a Grand Priestess and one hell of a powerful witch. She said you are a little package of magical dynamite, too." He paused, leaned forward, and kissed the tip of her nose then asked, "The whole dragon thing wasn't a surprise?"

"Well, it was a surprise that you're one and super cool to see you transform, but I've known since I was a little there are shifters of all kinds. I'm guessing that big Black Panther was a shifter, too? And with you?"

He nodded. "Yeah, that's Max. He's the King of the Big Cats. Our clan and his pride have been allies for years."

There was a lull in their conversation and Jace could tell they were both trying to decide what to say next. Unable to hold back, he said what he'd been thinking since the first time he'd recognized her as his. "I'm not sure how much you *know* about dragons but here is the simple truth. The legend says, there is one woman in all the world, created for each dragon shifter. She is the other half of his soul and that of his dragon's as well. The Universe made her especially for him and it is said she will bring light to his soul. I know it's true, not only because I've watched as other Guardsmen of our Force have each found their mate but also because I found you."

Clearing her throat and taking a deep breath she asked, "Are you sure?"

"Just as sure as I know the sun rises in the east and sets in the west. You are my mate and we are destined to be together, forever…in this life and the next."

He had no idea what she was thinking and refused to tap into their mating link to see. This was something she had to reconcile on her own. A flood of emotions crossed her face, but she never once broke eye contact with him. He took comfort in the fact that she was not hiding. They were facing whatever came next together.

Melanie squinted her eyes and tilted her head to the side like she was debating what to say next. Jace held his breath, praying she wasn't about to tell him to take a long walk off a short pier. It took a minute but finally she asked, "So that's why we can talk to each other…up here?" She tapped her temple.

Nodding, he chuckled. It wasn't the question he'd expected but knew it was the first of many. "Yes, ma'am. We call it mindspeak. All dragons have it once their initial transformation is complete. We can speak directly into the minds of anyone we have a bond of fealty or blood with and most importantly with our mates. It doesn't usually happen until after the official mating ceremony, but Kyra assures me that because of our combined magical ability, once our mating bond began, we were able to mindspeak."

"The mating bond is the reason I can feel things that you're feeling and know when you're close?"

"Right you are, *mo chroi'*."

"And you're not even the littlest bit freaked out that you're doomed to spend forever with the granddaughter of the *Grand Draoi* of the *Dorcha*? Not to mention, she doesn't really know how to use the power keg of magic inside her?'"

Jace opened himself completely to her, sending love and reassurance through their link. "I am not *doomed* to do anything. I am *destined* to spend the rest of my very long life with the best woman I've ever known. A woman that I love more than life itself."

He caught her chin gently between his thumb and index finger, refusing to let her look away from him. "She's not only gorgeous but has a heart the size of Texas, more compassion than Mother Theresa, and is smarter than Einstein."

Jace was rewarded with a small self-conscious smile. "You, Melanie Rose Whelan, are perfection personified. With you as my mate, I will want for nothing. I am honored and oh so very humbled to spend forever with you." Then he added, "And as far as using your magic goes, Kyra is more than willing to help you with anything you need."

One lone tear rolled down her cheek while Jace held his breath, waiting for her to respond. "Oh Jace, thank you so much. You have no idea how much this means to me. After almost twenty years of hiding, I finally belong. I love you, too, so very, very much."

Unable to stand the temptation of her pouty pink lips one second longer, he closed the distance between them, gently laid his lips to hers, and slowly kissed his mate. There was no rush, nothing to prove, just the perfect meeting of two souls that recognized the one that completed them in every way. He felt more alive, more complete, more of *everything* than ever before. The part of him that had been missing, the piece of his soul that made everything possible clicked into place. Too soon, Melanie broke away, breathless and dreamy-eyed. Jace's dragon followed suit and purred with contentment.

A gentle blush touched the apple of her cheeks when she noticed him watching her. She glanced at him through her thick, dark lashes before looking away and curling into his chest. He stroked her back, enjoying the complete solace of the moment. The man, the beast, and their mate were totally content. It was a perfect moment in time that Jace would remember forever.

"Mo ghra'?" He asked, happy Melanie already understood most of the ancient language.

"Yes?" She mumbled against his chest, stretching before propping up on her elbows and smiling.

"I made a promise to myself from the moment I found you missing. I swore that I would make you mine forever the minute I had you back in my arms."

He felt her holding her breath and watched as her eyes became as large and round as dinner plates. Shoving down the laughter that threatened to overflow, Jace pushed on. "Melanie Rose Whelan, will you do me the unparalleled honor of officially becoming my mate?"

If possible, her eyes got even larger, she then exhaled the breath she'd been holding and opened her mouth to speak. He barked out a laugh when all that crossed her lips was a tiny squeak. It took three tries but when she finally spoke, he thought he could fly without his dragon.

"Jace MacQuaid, there is nothing in this whole wide world that would make me happier than becoming your mate."

He whooped and hollered a 'Hell yeah' that had Liam, Dev, and Rory racing into the room. Before they could ask, he yelled, "She said yes! Can you believe that shit? She said yes!"

The three Guardsmen laughed and were in the process of congratulating the happy couple when a grumpy Royce and a smiling Kyra entered the room.

"What the hell, young'un? You couldn't wait until a decent hour to start celebrating." Royce grumbled.

"What he's really saying is…We couldn't be happier for you. When is the ceremony and what can we do to help?" Kyra added and the room erupted in laughter as the rest of the Guardsmen presently staying at Rory's house came straggling into the room.

Melanie looked at Jace, then at Kyra, then back to Jace with sheer panic in her eyes. "I have no idea how to plan a mating ceremony."

"Don't worry, *mo chroi'*. In dragon culture it's the man that does all the planning. I even get to pick out your gown."

"No way? That's great! I'm a total disaster when it comes to things like this."

"Not to worry. I got it covered."

"Hey, young'un, we doing this here or flying home for the festivities?" Royce asked, a little less grumpy than when he came in.

Looking back to Melanie, he answered. "Whatever Melanie wants, I'm good with, but I will admit to wanting her to be mine as quickly as possible."

"No pressure." Melanie joked. "Whatever you want to do is fine with me, Jace."

"Then here it is! Day after tomorrow we'll be officially mated."

"All right, young man, get your butt out of that bed and get to work. I'll sit with Melanie and answer any

questions she might have since Siobhan is an ocean away."
Kyra lightly clapped her hands together and made a
shooing motion with her hands toward the other
Guardsmen in the room. "Let's get the coffee going and
breakfast started while these two get ready for a busy day."

Stepping over the threshold, the little witch called
over her shoulder, "No dallying you two, we've got lots to
accomplish and two days to get it done."

Both Melanie and Jace laughed out loud as the door
clicked shut and the sounds of Kyra issuing orders
continued. In less than an hour they had both showered –
separately, much to Jace's chagrin – were dressed in fresh
clothes, and appeared at the **dining** room table just in time
to have breakfast.

Walking out the door with Liam and Rory in tow,
Jace looked over his shoulder one more time, taking in the
person he loved more than anything in the world. Their
eyes met, the electricity of their connection settled deep in
his heart, and he sighed as her voice floated through his
mind. *"I love you, Jace MacQuaid."*

CHAPTER EIGHT

The last two days had been crazy. Melanie learned so many things she never could've imagined about dragons, their origins and their customs. She wondered if she would ever remember it all. If that wasn't enough, tons of people had started to arrive, some she knew and some she didn't. She tried like hell to remember all their names but knew for sure she was going to screw up somewhere along the line.

Melanie nearly had a stroke when Jace dropped the bomb that his mother and two brothers were coming from the clan of his birth.

"What? Who's coming?" She spun around to face him.

"My mom and my brothers." He stated so matter of factly, she expected his sentence to end with 'duh'.

"Oh. Okay."

Walking across the room, Jace wound his fingers through hers and asked, "What's the matter, *m'fhíorghrá?*"

She smiled at the beautiful endearment, knowing full well he was her one true love as well. "Nothing. It's just for some reason I thought your family had passed like mine. It's just a shock, that's all."

"Okay, let's get one thing straight. That bullshit may work with everyone else but not with me. I want us to be honest about *everything* and that means *you tell me* when something is bothering you. It's my job to take care of it from there. Got it?" He kissed the tip of her nose, which eased the sting of his words, but Melanie had to make sure he understood who she was.

"While I appreciate your need to 'take care' of me and Kyra even prepared me for it, you need to realize that

I've been on my own for a long time. It's gonna take a while for me to not just take care of things on my own. But you are right, we do need to be honest with one another and I did hold back."

"I know you can take care of yourself. Hell, it's one of the million things I love about you. Now, out with it."

"I'm just afraid they won't like me." She spoke as fast as she could and mumbled, hoping Jace wouldn't hear but with his dragon hearing, he heard every word.

Lifting her into the air, he carried her to the chair by the window, sat down and placed her on his lap, facing sideways. He tenderly laid the tips of his fingers on her cheek, turning her head until they were facing one another. His smile was open and honest, making it hard for her to swallow past the lump in her throat. When he spoke, she could *feel* the love in his words.

"They are going to absolutely adore you. Mom, you can call her Jillian, loves to hug and will make all over you. Jonah, my older brother, will flirt with you until I want to rip his heart out, just to mess with me. Lastly, Jalen, who's five years younger than I am, will tell you every embarrassing story he can think of about our childhood. That's my family in a nutshell and you have nothing to worry about."

"But what about *my* family? What are they gonna think about the blood of a crazy, black magic *Grand Draoi* running through my veins?"

"My mom always said you can pick flowers and you can pick your seat, but you can't pick your relatives, so I'm sure they'll be just fine with it."

Melanie laughed out loud as her remaining anxiety melted away. Hugging Jace as tight as she could, she whispered, "Thank you."

"You're welcome, *mo chroi'.*" He lifted her off his lap and made sure she was steady on her feet before standing alongside her. A quick kiss and he was turning towards the door. "Now, I have tons of last minute things to get done. Not to mention the ladies were giving me grief for bothering you before the ceremony." With his hand on the knob, Jace turned and winked, then opened the door and said, "I love you more than the stars in the sky," before disappearing.

Wanting to make sure he knew she felt the same, she sent a message of her own through their mating bond. *"I loved you yesterday. I love you today. I'll love you tomorrow. Oh hell, I'll love you forever."* The warmth that filled her heart and soul let her know he'd heard and was just as happy as she was.

Kyra, Sam, Kyndel, Charlie, Anya, and Emma all came rushing into her room as soon as Jace had walked out the front door. Melanie was tickled that most of the mates from Jace's clan had come along with Rayne, Aaron, Rian, and Carrick to attend the reception after the mating ceremony, especially since only she, Jace, the Guardsmen of the Force, and the Elders could be at the ceremony. Melanie had asked several times if Jace was sure he didn't want to go home to get officially mated, but his response was always the same. "No way! I'm not letting *you* get away."

The doorbell rang while the ladies were doing her hair and helping her with her makeup. Kyra excused herself and returned just a few minutes later with a huge bouquet of spring flowers, a big white box with a bronze satin bow, and Hannah. Trying not to cry and mess up her newly applied makeup, Melanie motioned for her childhood friend to come closer. "You have to come here, crazy woman. They're trying to make me presentable."

With tears running down her cheeks, Hannah came right over, hugged her tight around the neck. "You are *always* presentable, goofball." Everyone in the room chuckled, then Hannah added, "I am so happy for you, Meli Rose."

"And I'm so happy you're safe and here with us." Melanie smiled.

Next came the flowers, Kyra placed them on a small table in front of the window closest to Melanie and handed her the card. *On your special day, we wish you all the love and happiness in the world. Sorry we couldn't be there with you and Jace: See you when you get home. All our love, Aidan, Grace, Ashton, Angus, and Sydney.* She completely understood that Grace and the twins were nowhere ready to travel and that Sydney had stayed to help with the new babies, but she was blown away by the couples' thoughtfulness.

Lastly, Kyra sat the white box on the bed. It was perfect timing as the others had just finished with her makeover. Rising, Melanie made her way to the bed, carefully untied the ribbon, laid the lid on the bed, and stood speechless as the strapless bodice of the gorgeous white gossamer gown shimmered and sparkled in the afternoon sun shining through the open window.

Picking it up, she awed at the expertly embroidered tiny bronze flames and diamond-like crystals that covered the entire top of the dress. Larger crystals cascaded from the cinched waistline to the bottom of the floor-length skirt. Turning towards the antique mirror that stood in the corner of the room, she held the dress in front of her, marveling at her own reflection.

"On my Heavens that is amazing." Sam breathed.

"Yes. It is stunning. Now, let's get you into it before your escorts get here." Kyndel winked.

In less than a minute, hands were coming at her from every direction. Jace's T-shirt that she'd used as a bathrobe was gently lifted over her head. "Arms up." Charlie instructed while she and Anya brought her mating gown over her head, careful not to disturb her hair or makeup.

Kyra **peeked** over her shoulder and began lacing up her bodice. "Tight enough? Can you still breathe?" The little witch teased.

Melanie nodded. As soon as Kyra had her all tied into her gown, Anya secured the wide bronze ribbon that **went** with the dress around her waist. Standing at her side, Devon's mate smiled sweetly. "You're just a vision, Mel."

"Give a spin, pretty lady." Emma chuckled from behind her.

Whirling like a princess at the ball, Melanie made two complete revolutions before stopping and facing the women that became more like sisters than friends to her in the last two days. Her heart filled with feeling of belonging and love completely foreign to her. Hannah walked towards her and placed the bronze satin slippers that accompanied her dress on the floor at her feet. Stepping into the shoes, she took a half turn and looked at the finished product now that she was made over from head to toe.

Looking good, kiddo. These ladies can work a serious makeover. They should start a salon.

"All right, Sadie, Sadie, soon to be married lady. I have it on good authority your escorts have just arrived." Kyra tapped her temple and Anya nodded in agreement.

Melanie followed as the ladies filed into the hallway and had just stepped into the living room when the doorbell sounded. Anya opened the door and there stood Devon and Royce dressed in surcoats reminiscent of Arthurian times, made from luxurious, bronze wool, trimmed in black braid with silver thread glittering throughout. She knew they matched the scales of Jace's dragon almost exactly from her brief introduction to the beast. On the front, there was an intricately embroidered picture depicting a dragon in flight. They each also wore a black, long-sleeved undershirt and pants, as well as knee high, polished black boots that shined in the afternoon sun.

The Guardsmen bowed, returned to standing, and announced in unison, "Your steed awaits, milady." Both men winked and all the women chuckled as Royce and Devon gently took her hands, placed them on their bent elbows, and led her to the black stallion with bronze and white ribbons braided into its mane.

Devon lifted her into the saddle and made sure she was steady enough to ride side saddle while Royce stroked the horse's nose and held him still. As soon as they were sure she was ready, the Guardsmen mounted their horses and started off towards the path that led to the beach. Royce at the front, Melanie in the middle with Devon bringing up the rear, they made short work of their trip to the shore.

When the sea wall came into view, Melanie also noticed a young Guardsman in training, Seth, whom she'd met at the lair. He stood at attention, dressed identically to Devon and Royce, holding an enormous bouquet of bronze roses. As soon as her feet touched the ground, the young man approached. Bowing low, he handed her the flowers, stood, and returned to his post at the top of the stone stairs that led to the beach.

She took the cream colored card elegantly embellished with her name, opened the envelope, and smiled at the message on the card. *Today I marry the best woman I've ever known. I love you more than the stars in the sky. Looking forward to forever with you. Love, J.*

Once again Devon and Royce offered her their bent elbows, but this time led her down the narrow stone steps to the beach. She removed her shoes as Kyra had instructed, thanked both older Guardsmen, and headed to the white wooden chair Royce had said was hers with Seth following close behind.

Making her way to her seat, she took in the elaborate preparations her mate had made to make their mating ceremony absolutely perfect. About ten yards from where she was to be seated stood a massive archway covered in bronze roses like the ones she carried, along with hundreds upon hundreds of bronze, silver, and white ribbons woven through the lattice work blowing in the sea breeze.

To the left was a large raised dais on which sat five ornate chairs resembling thrones. The platform, too, was decorated with bronze roses spilling from large ceramic urns wrapped in enormous white bows. There was also a large circle drawn in the sand with tiny white tea roses right in front of the platform.

Taking her seat, Melanie prepared to wait but was pleasantly surprised when less than two minutes later the four elders she'd met from Jace's clan and Rian, the Head Elder of the Blue Dragons and Royce's older brother, walked onto the platform, taking their places in the makeshift thrones.

Melanie then watched as the six men she knew were Guardsmen of the Force from Jace's clan appeared. They were all in the same dress uniforms as her escorts but with surcoats depicting what Jace had told her were the colors of their dragons. Rayne stood at the head of the line in flaming red. Royce was next, and had changed into his beautiful royal blue surcoat with green accents truly befitting the gentle giant that gave her mate as much trouble as he could. Next was Aaron, Charlie's mate, and one of the men she'd yet to get to know. He was dressed in silvery gray as was the man that stood next to him. She recognized him from the pictures in Jace's mind. This was the man that had been a traitor to his kin but now worked daily to redeem himself. Andrew was also Emma's mate and if anyone could turn someone around, it was the gentle jewelry artisan Melanie was proud to call friend.

The next in line was Lance, whose dress uniform was gold and black, he grinned and winked, letting her know the jokester had come prepared. Last in line was Devon, who had changed into his opalescent white surcoat.

106

From what Jace and Kyra had explained, she thought that was the end of the guest list for her mating ceremony, but the crunch of boots alerted her that there were more attendees on the way. From behind the dunes came Rory, Kellan, Declan, Lennox, Pearce, Brannoc, and Liam all dressed in their finery, as well. As she looked at the men her Jace held in high esteem, each man winked their approval and she grinned in response.

My family just keeps growing. Ain't love grand?

Looking around for the man she wanted to spend forever with, Melanie almost panicked until a glimpse of bronze fabric and the shine of black patented leather boots caught her eye. Turning in her seat, she could do little more than stare. Her pulse raced as she took in the man of her dreams. His short blond hair was blowing in the breeze and his brilliant blue eyes danced with mischief and so much love, she was humbled at the amazing mate the Universe had given to her.

Carrick's voice carried across the beach. "Long ago, when knights and dragons fought side by side for King and Country, it became apparent that dragon kin was no longer safe from those that would expose and destroy them. They sought to join with the knights that had fought so valiantly by their sides. Thus, through magic and the will of both dragon and knight, the Golden Fire Clan of the Dragon Shifters became a reality. It was through the joining of many different clans that we have become the strong and powerful Force we are today.

"We are here, in the place of importance to the couple, long blessed by our ancestors that have gone before us, to honor what the Universe put into place all those many years ago. To acknowledge and bless the mating of Jace Aaron MacQuaid to the one the Universe made for him, Melanie Rose Whelan. Will those seeking to witness this union please step forward."

All the Guardsmen from Jace's clan including Liam and Andrew stepped forward, then knelt in front of the Elders, and bowed their heads. Rayne stood, addressing the Elders, "We, the five of the MacLendon Force and those that will one day join our ranks, wish to witness and offer our blessing to the union of these two souls, two halves of the same whole. May they live long, fight hard, love harder, and produce many young to flourish when their souls have gone to the Heavens." He returned to his brethren, knelt, and again bowed his head.

Carrick began again, "Your witness and blessing have been acknowledged and accepted, MacLendon Force. Aherne Force, what say you?"

The six men of the Blue Thunder, all dressed in surcoats of varying shades of azure, stepped forward, knelt in front of the Elders, and bowed their heads. It was Rory that stood and addressed the Elders. "We, the six of the Aherne Force wish to offer our blessing to our brethren and his mate. May the Universe bless you. May you see your children's children. And may you know nothing but happiness from this moment forward." Rory returned to his brethren, knelt, and bowed his head.

"Your blessing is most welcome, Aherne Force," Carrick acknowledged. All the Guardsmen stood in unison and returned to their places next to the platform.

"Jace MacQuiad, you may go to your mate and escort her to the center of the Blessed Circle." No sooner had the words been spoken than Jace was standing in front of Melanie.

He took her roses in one hand and pulled her to standing with the other. Reaching around, he placed the roses on the chair she'd just vacated, kissed her cheek, and then led her to the center of the circle drawn with tiny white roses.

"The bronze dragons were forged from the hard core of the Earth. They are powerful, solid dragons that possess especially hard scales and because of this, are often referred to as the 'Warrior Dragons'. Carrick spoke with authority.

"They are protective to a fault and will fight to the death to defend those they hold dear. They seek justice at all turns. They have meticulous and ambitious attitudes and use a combination of their minds and hearts to make all decisions. They love hard, strong, and endlessly. They never lose faith in whom or what they believe in. To mate a bronze dragon is to accept all that they are and honor the power shared between mates.

"Now is the time of the marking. May the Universe continue to bless you and yours all the days of your lives together."

The Elders left the beach as the Guardsmen positioned bamboo panels around the couple, giving them privacy where before there had been none. In a flash the dragons were gone.

Staring at the man she loved more than her own life, Melanie felt his love deep in her soul. He smiled that smile that made her weak in the knees and let her know he'd heard her thoughts and that he felt exactly the same way.

The longer they stared at one another, the more brilliant his eyes became until she realized they were glowing.

Jace lowered his mouth to hers, stopping just as their lips touched, and whispered, *"Tá tú mo ghrá eternal. Ta' mo chroi istigh ionat,"* before capturing her lips with his.

Melanie could feel Jace and his dragon *everywhere*. She was consumed with a heat that laid her open…body, heart, and soul to her mate.

A sting on the left side of her neck caused her try to pull back. Jace held her close, left her lips, and trailed kisses across her jaw and down her neck, reaching the tender spot that had stung only a moment before. He licked and sucked the offending area until all thoughts of anything but their naked bodies loving one another were banished from her mind.

She placed her hands on either side of his face and pulled his mouth to hers, kissing him until they were both again breathless. Jace pulled back and it was then that she saw the glint of mischief in his eyes. Grinning a sneaky grin of her own, she asked, "What's going on in that beautiful mind of yours, Mr. MacQuaid?"

"So many, many things, Mrs. MacQuaid."

She loved the sound of her new name on his lips and leaned in to give him a kiss, but he pulled back. "I want nothing more than to kiss you *everywhere* for every moment of the rest of our lives, but we have a reception to go to and I have a surprise for you." Jace waggled his eyebrows. Melanie laughed out loud.

Picking her up while she still giggled, Jace wound around the bamboo panels and using his enhanced speed, took her up the stairs and across a tiny meadow to a blanket spread out under a large oak tree with a picnic basket sitting in the center. Kissing her behind the ear, he gently sat her on the blanket before opening the basket and joining her.

In the blink of an eye, Jace's hand removed a small velvet box from the bin and set it in her hands. Melanie looked from him to the box and back again. "But I didn't get you anything."

"Oh, but you did, Mrs. MacQuaid. You gave me your heart and there's nothing more in all the world I could ever want."

Taking a deep breath to keep from crying and ruining her makeup, she opened the small hinged box and stared at its contents, completely dumbfounded. There, highlighted by the soft bronze velvet, was a thick platinum band with a tiny bronze bell hanging from an intricate Claddagh setting.

Jace lifted the ring from its velvet pillow and the bell tinkled like the wings of the fairies she played with as a child. Melanie placed her hand in her mate's outstretched palm. As soon as their skin touched, the jolt of electricity she'd come to associate with Jace zipped through her body and landed deep in her womb, making her wish they could skip the reception.

Having heard her thoughts, Jace barked out a laugh and agreed. His expression switched to thoughtful in the blink of an eye and with his smooth baritone voice he spoke directly into her mind. *"With this ring I thee wed. Wear it as symbol of our love and commitment. May this ring be blessed so that he who gives it and she who wears it may abide in peace and continue to love beyond life's end."* Then he slipped the ring onto her finger.

The tears she had been fighting to hold back all day began to fall. "Hey there. No tears. Today's a happy day." Jace pulled her onto his lap and placed butterfly kisses on her cheeks and forehead, drying her tears as he went.

"And these are happy tears, Jace. You make me so very, very happy."

CHAPTER NINE

He had been officially mated to Melanie for exactly three hours and they had yet to be alone. Both the man and his dragon were at the end of their proverbial rope. It was time to carry her back to Rory's house and consummate their mating before Jace spontaneously combusted.

She'd met his mother and brothers, who loved her at first sight, just like he knew they would. They'd cut the cake, danced all the dances, and accepted congratulations from people he wasn't even sure he knew. It was time to get the hell outta dodge and he was going to make it happen.

Making his way across the makeshift dance floor, he finally found his wayward mate chatting with the other ladies. "Oh no, he's got that look." Kyra teased.

"Yep, he sure does." Kyndel winked. "Guess we better say goodnight." She laughed, closely followed by everyone at the table.

Jace knew he should be more discreet but that course of action had flown out the window about two and half hours ago. He wanted Melanie so bad, he'd suffer embarrassment and harassment for years to come just to be alone with her. "Guess the gig is up," he confessed while lifting Melanie into his arms.

"Jace! Put me down!"

"Oh, I plan to, in about ninety seconds." The words were barely out of his mouth before they were speeding away, stopping only when they were on the porch of Rory's house. The older Guardsman had graciously moved out of his home and taken his other houseguests for the duration of their stay, a gift Jace would make sure was repaid.

"I hear there's a human custom where the man carries his mate over the threshold," Jace commented, holding onto his composure by the thinnest thread.

"Yes…there is."

Slowly and deliberately, Jace lowered his lips towards hers, stopping right before they touched. "Then we're going to do this right." He growled just as their lips met.

He kissed her with all that he was, pouring his undying love into her so that she would never doubt how truly special she was to him. He stepped over the threshold, slammed the door shut, and tore through the house like a man possessed.

Reaching the bedroom, he gently laid her on the soft down of the white eyelet comforter he'd placed on the bed earlier in the day. Unable to be even a few inches from his mate, Jace settled on top of Melanie, holding his weight on his forearms positioned beside her head.

When her legs went around his waist bathing his throbbing erection in her delicious heat, he thanked the Heavens for the strategically placed slits on both sides of her gown.

Jace rolled his hips, holding her body captive, loving the look of complete abandon on her face. His hands felt their way across her hips, up her ribs, and rested lightly at the sides of her breasts, enjoying their fullness. His thumbs teased the area close to her nipples through her dress. He smirked as Melanie arched her back, trying to force his touch. He hadn't meant to torture her but had to admit watching his mate loving his touch had just become his new favorite pastime.

Unable to stand his own torment a moment longer, he reached around her body, quickly locating the ribbon that held her bodice to her chest. Lifting her into a sitting position, he kissed and tasted along her collarbone, making short work of the satin cord that was keeping her dress in place. One pull and the bodice fell. His mouth watered as her voluptuous breasts and berry-colored nipples were revealed. Licking across first one and then the other of her hardened peaks, he was rewarded with an "Oh my God, Jace…please…*please* never stop," moaned from low in her throat.

Needing to leave no part of his mate untouched, Jace took the nipple between his lips, teasing it with his teeth and tongue until Melanie bowed her back, pushing more of her breast into his mouth, and begging him to never stop.

The scent of dianthus in the summer sun filled the room as he drove Melanie's arousal higher and higher. His dragon pushed and roared in his head, demanding to taste their mate's nectar. Assuring the beast they would soon taste all of her, he continued his seduction. Releasing her nipple, Jace latched onto the other, working her dress down her body and over her beautifully rounded hips. His fingers slowed as the lace of her underwear teased his fingertips.

He left her nipple, kissing the valley between her breasts, tasting and marking every inch he could reach of her erotically curvy body. He reached the silk of her panties with his lips and inhaled long and deep. Melanie's wonderfully unique scent left him unable to resist any longer. He knelt between her thighs, dragging the gown from her body and throwing the offending garment over his shoulder as soon as her feet slipped free. Ripping the tiny silk strings of her panties, they followed her dress, and finally his Melanie was gloriously naked and open to do with as he pleased.

She was absolutely stunning. Truly the most magnificent creature he's ever laid eyes on. As slowly as his need to be inside her would allow, he took in every inch of her glorious body. Jace started with the deep wine polish that covered her toes, up her shapely legs that would soon be wrapped around his body in ways most people only imagined, to her soft thighs he'd dreamt of having under his head from the first time he'd watched her walk away from him. Her rounded stomach, along with all her curves, begged to be loved over and over again.

"Jace?" His name on her lips drew his gaze.

"Yes, *mo ghra*?" He crooned, massaging her thighs, making sure to brush the outer lips of her pussy every chance he could get. The way her hips jumped at every touch made his cock jump in his pants.

"Jace…I want…No, I *need*…." She panted.

"What is it you need, *mo chroi*?" He teased, running his index finger up and down her slit, already wet with the proof of her arousal.

Her breathing grew more ragged and her head thrashed from side to side as she begged for him to continue. Jace marveled at the vision of Melanie in the throes of passion, her head thrown back, her eyes closed tight, her mouth open as she called his name like a prayer to the Heavens.

"I…Jace…Oh my…Jace…yes!" She wailed as he pushed through her folds and teased her opening, the juices of her arousal wetting his hand. Her pussy contracted around the tip of his finger, attempting to pull his digit farther into her warm wet passage. Adding another finger, he began gliding them in and out, her honey providing the perfect lubrication. His thumb drew lazy circles around her swollen clit while his fingers drove her higher. Every few swipes he bent his fingers so the tips would gently brush the very special bundle of nerves that made Melanie wild with pleasure.

Needing to taste her more than he needed his next breath, he pulled out his fingers and answered her whine at the loss by driving his tongue into her pussy as far as he could reach. Her taste exploded on his tongue, flashes of light bursting before his eyes. He devoured Melanie like a starving man, swallowing every drop of nectar that flowed from her. The more his tongue moved within her, the more of her he drank in until he felt drunk. Her legs came over his shoulders, closing around his head, making breathing almost impossible, and still he consumed all she had to give.

He felt her tense just a second before her orgasm overtook her. Screaming his name, she came on his tongue, filling his mouth until her juices ran down his chin. He continued to lick and massage as she came back to earth.

Looking up, he found her smiling a lazy smile and gazing at him through passion-filled eyes. His only thought was to keep that exact look on her face for the rest of their lives together.

His cock pulsed against his zipper and it was then that he realized he was still completely dressed. Not wanting to leave his place between her thighs but needing to feel her skin against his, Jace stood in one fluid motion, threw off his surcoat, tore the black long-sleeved T-shirt over his head, and had his pants kicked in the corner as quickly as possible.

Climbing onto the bed, he held himself above Melanie, only a few inches separating their lips. Ever so slowly, he slid into her warm, wet channel. Inch by inch, he joined with his mate, shaking with the effort it took to go slow. Every contraction of her inner muscles pulled him farther into her body, milked his cock, and begged him to move faster. Summoning all his control, Jace held back. Sweat covered his chest and ran down his back.

Melanie was so wet and ready, her excitement growing so quickly that her juices flowed freely from her pussy, puddling between them. When he was seated completely within her, he held completely still, reveling in the feel of his mate wrapped so tightly around his cock. He watched her face, eyes closed in passion, sweat dotting her upper lip, and lips parted while she panted. "Look at me, mo *ghra'*. Look at the man that will love with all that is in this life and the next."

Melanie's eyes flew open. Jace felt the electricity only they could create sizzling stronger and brighter. She wrapped her legs around his waist and held tight as he began to casually slide in and out of her. She met him stroke for stroke. Their pace accelerated until he was pistoning in and out of her dripping channel, driving them both to the release they so desperately needed.

She grabbed his shoulders, her manicured nails biting into his skin as she crushed her chest to his. The feel of her pebbled nipples rubbing against his chest created a friction he thought would set them ablaze. Shifting his hips, he caused his pelvis to bump her clit and his cock to rub the sensitive bundle of nerves atop her channel with every stroke. He could feel her orgasm building, bringing them both to the edge of something bigger and better than either had ever imagined.

Buried deep inside his mate, Jace felt her muscles contract even more tightly around him until he was sure they had become one in body, just as they already were in spirit.

"Trust me, *mo chroi'*, let go and trust me. You'll never be alone again," he groaned and thrust into her so hard and fast he bumped her cervix. The exquisite sensation undid them both.

Melanie and Jace came with such force their bodies shook and it was hard to stay conscious. He had no clue if the shouting he heard was his or hers or both. He watched as his exquisite mate floated back to earth and could not resist placing butterfly kisses on her face and neck. He rolled to the side taking her with him, and lovingly placed her across his body, enjoying that she was boneless and spent, and he had made her that way. A peace he'd never known flowed between them. She opened her eyes and he was once again hopelessly lost to the one the Universe made for him. Jace knew there would never come a day when he would not need this woman with every fiber of his being.

Hours later they lay completely exhausted, her head on his chest, their legs intertwined while their sweat soaked bodies cooled from their lovemaking. Her hand rubbed tiny circles on his chest, causing the bell on her ring to tinkle almost continually.

Sitting up, he positioned Melanie on his lap, kissing her finger above and below her ring. "Emma made this ring especially for you, even before I'd worked up the nerve to speak to you for the first time."

"Really?"

"Really. The bell is made out of one of my dragon's scales."

"Oh, Jace, that's amazing, but why a bell?"

"Have you never heard the old saying?"

"I don't remember one about a bell." She furrowed her brow and he could tell she was trying to recall one.

Pulling her tight to his chest, he looked deep into her eyes as he lowered his lips to hers. As soon as they touched, he answered in the way of mates. *"Every time a dragon kisses his mate, a bell rings. And I really hope you like the sound our little bell makes because I plan to kiss you every minute of every day."*

Melanie's chuckle sounded in his head, quickly followed by a sigh that said she was onboard with his plan for the future.

"I love you more than the stars in the sky, Melanie Rose MacQuaid."

"Yesterday, today, and tomorrow. I'll love you forever, Jace MacQuaid. Just keep this bell ringing."

EPILOGUE

How could he not have seen that his one and only heir was fated to mate a dragon shifter? And not just any dragon shifter but one of the Dragon Guardsmen of legend. Had he known, he could have placed wards specific to the giant winged warriors. He could have taken her anywhere but to his beloved coven, to the home of his followers. Melanie was the
one of legend and now she was ensconced in a dragon clan, mated to a shifter.

It wasn't that he cared so much about the people themselves, but the sheer numbers and generations of *Dorcha* he had lost was something he didn't have the time to regain. The number of witches and wizards and lineage coupled with the influence of the homeland of their founders had been a huge source of power for the *Grand Draoi* and in one fell swoop he'd lost all of it.

The saving grace had been his foresight to have Soren and Mara keep the Grand Priestess on the other side of the mountain. At least they were able to continue their pursuit to 'persuade' Calysta to give them the location of the Thanatos spell. Their ability to bring the Dark Lord back to Earth would secure Cleland's place of power and give him the immortality he so desperately desired.

Of course, he also a backup plan for his backup plan. Hidden inside the soul of one of his followers was a spell of his own design. An incantation that if worked by him and him alone would bring all the dark magic practitioners in the world together for the purpose of opening the Hell Mouth to the *Demon ar ríchathaoir.* Once the spell was activated and its courier sacrificed, the *Draoi* would be able to bring a piece of Hell to the Earth. Its inhabitants would be beholden to him, servants that would then help him find Thanatos.

He wondered what his precious Meli Rose would do if she knew her oldest and closest friend carried the ritual that could destroy the world.

~~*~*~*~*~*~*

The last week had been utter torture, every time he saw her it was as if he'd been punched in the gut. His heart raced, his blood felt as if it was boiling in his veins, and his dragon howled with the need to be near her. It wasn't as if Liam hadn't recognized her as his mate the moment he saw her standing in the shadows, trying to remain unseen when they'd rushed in to save Melanie. Of course he had. It had been just like all the stories he'd heard growing up.

He'd seen the golden highlights of her strawberry-blonde hair glistening in the firelight and it was obvious. When the seductively soft scent of Angel's trumpets with their light lemony overtones had invaded his senses, Liam Drennan just knew she was the one the Universe had made for him and him alone.

The few times he'd decided to go to her something had pushed him away, made it impossible for him to get near her. He'd felt the mating call, even sensed the beginning of the mating bond, but something dark almost evil within *her* had shut it down and denied him access to his mate. There was something about Hannah McKennon that didn't add up.

Now, all Liam had to do was figure out how to tell his friend's mate that her best friend had something evil living inside her, attempting to control her. Who was he kidding? There was no way this was going to end well for anyone involved.

Oh great! Just another day in paradise.

Also by Julia Mills
~~*~*~*~*~*

Her Dragon to Slay, Dragon Guard Series #1
Her Dragon's Fire, Dragon Guard Series #2
Haunted by Her Dragon, Dragon Guard Series #3
For the Love of Her Dragon, Dragon Guard Series #4
Saved by Her Dragon, Dragon Guard #5
Only for Her Dragon, Dragon Guard #6
Fighting for Her Dragon, Dragon Guard #7
***

Her Love, Her Dragon: The Saga Begins, Dragon Guard Prequel

CPSIA information can be obtained
at www.ICGtesting.com
Printed in the USA
LVHW081524280319
612180LV00032B/595/P